The Karris Family

The Karris Family

Ruhani K. Chhabra

Library of Congress Control Number:		2015917409
ISBN:	Hardcover	978-1-5144-1790-4
	Softcover	978-1-5144-1789-8
	eBook	978-1-5144-1788-1

Print information available on the last page.

Rev. date: 11/10/2015

To order additional copies of this book, contact:
Xlibris
1-888-795-4274
www.Xlibris.com
Orders@Xlibris.com
720839

CONTENTS

Introduction

Change

You may be thinking, what's the big deal about change?

Well, my friends, *it is a big deal.*

Trust me, just do. Honestly, this unfriendly change made my life complex. Very, very complex.

Let me tell you one thing: change can be good or bad.

I used to watch these movies where happy endings always come even if there is change or bad, problematic situations.

Well, in my life, it is definitely *not* like a film. You can probably guess that already.

After my younger sister, Daisy, was born, things changed in my house. A lot.

My older sister, Allison, started her last year in middle school. She became more interested in makeup and started behaving rudely to Mom and Dad.

My older brother, Fred, started his junior year in high school. He thought he was the king, when he really was nothing. Maybe I'm being too harsh, but you haven't seen my family.

My dad got demoted from his job, so he worked even harder in the office to get back in his previous role or higher. Yep, we had money problems. Or as adults call it, financial crisis.

My mom was definitely more stressed than before, and Daisy was very stubborn, so she had to take care of her pretty much 24-7. Also, she worked part-time as a nurse.

How would I survive with all these difficult changes in my family? Me, Leah Karris? Puny fifth grader, smaller and thinner than others in my class? Big glasses, ugly hazel-brown eyes, and knotty short brown hair to my neck? You'll be surprised how I did.

Chapter 1: Mountain Out of a Molehill

I woke up one early morning from sounds of *fighting* of my mother and older sister, Allison.

I tumbled out of bed, landing on my fuzzy rug.

Out of the blue, Allison, came in my room.

"Mrs. Mary Karris wants you to go eat breakfast," she said irritably. Allison's brown eyes and hair were boring like mine except she had blond highlights.

"Mrs. Mary Karris? What's up with that? Why don't you just say *Mom*?" I snapped back in the same tone.

"Listen, twerp, I don't have time to explain to you what happened when Mrs. Mary Karris didn't let me go to the party at Brooklyn's house, so she's definitely not my mom."

"I thought you didn't have time to explain to me?" I asked like I cared.

"Just go eat breakfast and be quiet, scrawny chicken legs, go."

I quickly brushed my hair and put on a hideous brown hand-me-down sweater from Allison. It smelled like fish and potatoes.

I entered the kitchen. Fred was texting. Dad was working. Mom was cooking.

They didn't notice me until I sat on the table and "accidentally" dropped my spoon.

"Good morning, Leah," Mom said as she fried the eggs. There were dark circles around her eyes and stress pimples on her face. "Would you like bacon and eggs or cereal?"

"Cereal. But, Mom, why is Allison so mad at you?"

"You know her. Always making a mountain out of a molehill."

Chapter 2: My School Troubles

I missed the bus that day, so I had to walk to school. I was late because, unfortunately, I was not the fastest runner or walker.

When I entered Mrs. Albright's fifth-grade classroom, I was eight minutes late. I didn't want to get in class because everyone would be staring at me, but I finally opened the space-gray door. It was so windy that a paper flew out of the door. I thought it was a tiny white bird and I screamed really loud.

"Leah Karris! What are you doing? Trying to distract the class?" Mrs. Albright scolded.

"Mrs. Albright, I thought that I saw a bird and I screamed so—"

"Leah, I think you need some time to settle down. Go ahead and sit outside until you are ready."

I grumbled to myself and went out the door. This was one of the reasons I didn't like Mrs. Albright. She didn't let me explain what really happened, and she just jumped to conclusions.

I sat on the freezing-cold bench outside of Mrs. Albright's classroom. Mrs. Albright was middle-aged and had orange hair with a couple of gray streaks. She wore pantsuits and lots of red lipstick and had yellow teeth like a banana peel. On the first day of school, when I saw Mrs. Albright, I thought she should brush her teeth more. I guess I should not suggest that to her; one, I would get in trouble, and two, I didn't brush my teeth that often myself. Then I would be acting like a hypocrite. And I hate hypocrites.

Angela Hartman, the teacher's pet and know-it-all, came outside. Her blond curls bounced, and her blue eyes shone with excitement, like she was the first person to set foot on Mars.

"Mrs. Albright says to come inside. And I—I mean we—I mean Mrs. Albright doesn't expect this type of behavior again," she said in a harsh voice.

I rolled my eyes. I felt angry the minute she said those lines. "Why would I want to come inside? Tell her that I don't want to go in. And get out of my face!" I said with a finger pointing at her face.

"Huh? You can't *say* and *do* that!"

"Well, watch me," I said, crossing my arms.

"I'm telling!" she said, running to the room.

Mrs. Albright didn't come. Angela didn't come.

The recess bell rang. Kids zoomed out the door and looked at me like I was crazy. Even Zoe Hawk was giving a mean look, and I couldn't believe that she was my friend until second grade, when she started gossiping about me and people started to dislike me. Finally, Mrs. Albright came out the door. "Leah, if you want to continue with your behavior, go ahead and walk to Mr. Holcomb's office." She glared at me with her eyes wide open like a fish.

I was silent. Instead, I looked at the ground and counted the ants. *One, two, three,* I thought.

"Well, Leah?" Mrs. Albright said.

"Mrs. Albright, I really didn't mean to yell that loudly. See, the thing was—"

"I don't care about that, Leah. All I want to know is what you want to do. Do you want to continue doing this behavior or come inside?"

"I wasn't doing anything. First of all, I just said that I want to stay outside. How is that bad? I don't understand," I uttered in the same kind of tone.

Mrs. Albright took a deep breath and told me to go to Mr. Holcomb's office. I had been there before, just to give the attendance record. When I reached the office Ms. Amy, the nicest secretary in the world, was sitting on her desk, typing on the computer.

The only problem was that Ms. Amy only came when Mrs. Lean (also known as Mrs. Mean) was sick.

"Hi there, Leah! What's going on? Why are you here?" she asked.

I muttered, "I have a meeting with Mr. Holcomb."

Mrs. Lean, forty years old and grumpy, would usually ask why, and then she would say under her breath "Rotten kid" or talk behind my back to other teachers. Ms. Amy, on the other hand, who was young and cheerful, didn't say anything.

"'Kay, honey, knock on Mr. Holcomb's door," Ms. Amy said, looking back at the computer.

I took a deep breath and knocked on the door.

Chapter 3: Mr. Holcomb's Office

Mr. Holcomb opened the door. He had gray and wispy hair and wore a dull striped tie with a black suit.

"Ah, Leah Karris, I've been expecting you," he said in a deep, low voice. "Sit, sit over there."

I nervously took a seat in a green armchair.

As I settled down, I took a look at his office. There was a silvery giraffe statue near his desk adjacent to a bookshelf filled with books. On his desk was a picture frame of two girls and Mr. Holcomb. I figured this was Mr. Holcomb's wife and daughter. The wall was painted completely white, like snow.

He sipped some coffee and looked at me. "So, Leah, Mrs. Albright told me that you had screamed and were incredibly rude. Is that true?"

I explained everything to him but didn't mention the episode with Angela and Mrs. Albright.

"Uh-huh. Why didn't you tell Mrs. Albright that?"

"I tried, but she didn't listen."

"Okay, but as Mrs. Albright told me, why were you being rude to your fellow Angela Hartman?" asked Mr. Holcomb.

I stopped dead. He got me there. What excuse did I have for this? I wanted to tell everything about little Ms. Bossy Angela and her nasty mouth. Instead, I just stayed silent and studied my lap.

"Leah? Why were you rude? You know the school rules. Do not be rude or disrespectful. 'Get out of my face' is not a very good thing to say."

I didn't know what to say, so I shrugged.

"All right then. Your parents will be informed about this. Also, I'm sorry, Leah, but this behavior is unacceptable in Cherry City Elementary School."

He handed me a detention slip and took another sip of his steaming coffee from his big mug.

I got up from the chair and walked out of Mr. Holcomb's office very angry. At that time, I thought that he deserved to be in a retirement home.

Chapter 4: The Painfully Long Day

The rest of the day was painfully long. Mrs. Albright kept glaring at me all through algebra.

Finally, the bell rang. Phew! I wanted to head home immediately, but I had detention. I trudged to the detention room.

Mrs. Lean was there on the desk. "What happened to Ms. Amy?" I blurted out the minute I saw her.

Mrs. Lean gazed at me with mad eyes, as if she wanted to eat me up. She certainly did look like a Mrs. Mean.

"Scram, kid," she snapped.

"I have detention."

"Why?"

I wanted to say that it was none of her business, but I couldn't afford another detention, so I just shrugged.

"Ugh, let me talk to Mr. Holcomb." Mrs. Lean left the room.

When she came back in, she looked cheerful. "You will do your detention on Saturday. Understood?" she said. "And you'll be sitting with Mr. Crows instead of me."

I was pretty happy when she said that because the last thing I wanted to do was sit with Mrs. Lean for half an hour. Mr. Crows was my fourth-grade teacher. He was okay, I guess.

Chapter 5: The Phone Call

I ran home. Mom would probably ground me for the weekend, but who cares? I had no friends anyway. I was just about to push the door open and get a snack, like some celery sticks and peanut butter, but I heard Mom talking to Uncle Ray. "Yes, yes, Ray, but unfortunately, Steve and I do not have the time to visit you all in New York for the ball drop."

"Send the kids then, Mary," I heard Uncle Ray say, because the telephone was on speaker.

"We'll see. I'll call you later." She hung up.

I entered my home.

She looked at me like she was furious but puzzled. I felt she was looking at me like that because she thought I was the dumbest child in her household. My cheeks got hot.

Mom's lips curled into a straight line. "Why did I get a call from your school saying—"

"Mom, I really didn't do anything. I'll explain to you if you tell me what Uncle Ray was saying."

Mom sighed. "Uncle Ray wants us to go visit his family in New York and join them for the new year ball drop. It would be nice to see your Aunt Denise and Uncle Ray and your cousins, Nelly and Eric. We haven't seen them in a while. But the thing is, your father and I have been so busy since he got demoted that we don't have the time. Daisy's too young. I don't know if Allison and Fred would want to go. And I don't think how the three of you can go alone."

"Of course we can! Fred's pretty much like an adult, and so is Allison. And I'm almost eleven!"

"We'll see, Leah," she answered quickly. Which obviously meant probably not. "Now why don't you tell me what happened at school." But then Mom got a text from Allison that read, "Mom I'm gonna go on a local bus, don't pick me up, I'm fine so don't freak out or anything. LOL."

"Hold that thought," she said. "This girl drives me crazy." My mother rang Allison and started yelling at her over the phone.

I pushed back my chair to get some milk and chocolate biscuits (the peanut butter and celery sticks were finished), but then I felt rage all over me. Mom being so busy with Allison and Daisy. Allison being so busy with herself. Fred being so busy with schoolwork and friends that I can't even see his face. Dad being so busy with work. Nobody cared about me! I'm just an unwanted child.

I bet if I ran away, they wouldn't even notice for hours, maybe days. That's when I decided to do an experiment. I remembered that Mr. Jackson, my science teacher, had told us that the science fair was coming up and we had to come up with some kind of experiment. So , I thought, why don't I try doing an experiment on my real life? But then I realized how would that be considered for science fair, when it is not related to science. I made up mind that I will do this for myself and not the science fair.

I rushed to my room, which was painted light green. Daisy came toddling over to me. "I can't play now, Daisy, I'm working," I said, kissing her little cheek.

I wrote on the paper:

Problem: My parents and family don't notice me.

Observation: They tend to ignore me, I think on accident.

Hypothesis: If I go away for a while, they wouldn't notice.

All I had to do was wait for Allison, Fred, and Dad to come home. Then I could do my experiment.

Chapter 6: Sneaking Out

Time arrived when I had to put my experiment into action. It was four thirty when Allison came back, whining and complaining, as usual. Fred came at five, bragging about an A he got in chemistry. Dad came home the latest, at six forty-five. Now, I thought, was the best time for me to sneak out.

But I would actually be happy if my family noticed. Fred and Allison didn't notice me when they came back. Dad didn't either until I went in the room.

"Supper is in ten minutes," Mom called from the kitchen. I observed my family as Mom made dinner. Fred was sitting on the kitchen table, reading his textbooks. Allison was still doing her homework. Dad was looking like he was writing an e-mail saying that he had gotten extra money for working overtime.

No one said one peep. I tried to talk while I set the table, as I always did those days.

"Mom, aren't you going to tell everyone about Uncle Ray's phone call?" I said, as Mom put spoons on our plates.

"Oh, yes!" Mom said. "Today Ray said that we should go to the ball drop with him and Denise and their children." She put vegetables on everyone's plates.

"I don't know, Mary," Dad responded, looking up from his computer.

"And, I'm going to Mexico with Sondra," Allison blurted in.

"Since when are you going to Mexico, young lady? You never told me," Dad snapped as he looked up from his computer and stopped typing.

"I have to study, and I have ten Sweet Sixteens to go to," Fred interjected before Allison could say anything about her going to Mexico. Mom had convinced Fred to eat dinner with us. He agreed on the condition that if he didn't finish his food in fifteen minutes, he could take it upstairs to his room.

"Can't I go as an unaccompanied minor, Mom?" I begged. "Please, please, please!"

"*Enough*," she bellowed. "Stop talking at the same time, it gives me a headache."

Dad replied, "Why don't we let Leah go? I mean, I don't see any harm in that. Wait, speaking about Leah, why did I get a call from her school stating that she went to the principal's office—"

I explained everything very fast to get it over with. Allison smirked and did a cough that sounded like "idiot."

"Allison, eat your green beans," Dad said.

"Yeah, brat," I remarked, sticking my tongue out.

"Leah . . ." Mom gave me a look that said you-are-already-in-trouble-be-quiet-and-eat-your-dinner.

"Anyways, it would be a good idea for me to go to New York. I barely ever see Nelly and Eric," I said, looking up from my baked potato and onions.

"How much is the cost of the ticket?" Dad questioned.

"Two hundred sixty-four dollars for a UM," Mom answered.

I gasped at how much money that was and dropped my broccoli (on purpose). "Oops."

"Leah, pick that up right now!" my mother boomed.

"May I be excused?"

"Yes, go. We will talk about your punishment later." Just then, a heated argument between Mom and Allison started about her going to Mexico. Fred and Dad started bickering on something about a new computer.

Perfect time to sneak out, I thought. I quickly got my coat and boots and beaded purse with ten dollars inside. I headed out the back door. Daisy started to cry when she saw me go. I guess she was the only one who noticed. Mom gave her a milk bottle, and she calmed down. Daisy watched me leave silently from the back door.

The cold wind stung my eyes. I had no friends, so where would I go? Pete's Pizzeria was still open. Since I barely ate dinner, I was hungry. I had ten bucks in my bag. I could buy at least a couple of breadsticks. I walked two blocks to the pizza place.

Chapter 7: Pete's Pizzeria

Pete was in the kitchen, so his daughter, Maria, took my order. "Hi. What can I get you?" she asked, very surprised since it was very late.

"Oh, just two breadsticks."

"That'll be one ninety-nine, please."

"How much does a small cheese pizza cost?"

"Three fifty-five."

"I'll have both!" I exclaimed on the remarkably low prices, handing her the money. As I sat down on the table, I looked at the decor. There was a yellow wall with paint chipping out with a quote that said, "You can never have too much pizza." There were ten tables, but only mine was occupied.

As Maria handed me the pizza and breadsticks, I had never tasted anything so good. Yum! It didn't just taste cheesy; it tasted a bit spicy and a bit salty.

She smiled at my happy face.

"This," I said between chews on the delicious pizza, "is amazing."

"We tend to put Mexican spices and sometimes vegetables in our pizza, but we mix it inside the dough so people can't see them. We're going to add rice and beans to the menu soon," Maria spoke.

Then I noticed a cross street shop named 'Hartman's Pizza'. It had lots of rush. I had tried it before, and it wasn't tasty at all. They put caviar on pizza, which cost a lot. Worst of all, my snotty classmate Angela Hartman's dad owned the place, so she was also there sometimes.

When Maria saw me looking at Hartman's Pizza, she said, "Yeah, ever since Hartman's Pizza opened, business has been slow, so we thought of reducing the prices."

"People are so stupid," I replied, taking a sip of water.

"Well, I wish we had more members in our family working. My brother Mateo's in Stanford University with a full scholarship. But the Hartman Pizza family members work together and make way more money. Hey, do you know the Karris family? I learnt that they have lots of money too. Allison Karris is in my class and said that Frank—no Fred, Allison's older brother—also has a full scholarship to go to Princeton. Allison also said she was super rich and she said she has Prada shoes. I also heard Allison saying that she had a new cute baby sister named D-D—" Maria scratched her chin while she tried to remember the name.

"Daisy." My face was blank, and so was my tone.

"You know the Karris family?" her voice became excited.

"No, I'm part of the Karris family." I blinked and had nothing else to say.

"Um . . . are you—"

"Leah."

"Oh, I completely forgot about that!" Maria said with a nervous chuckle. Obviously Allison had not even mentioned me. My older sister was a brat, a liar, and a cheater. *We were not rich.*

Maria tried changing the subject. "Why are you out so late, Leah?"

"I'm doing an experiment about whether my family notices or not while I'm out."

"Of course they did!" she scolded. "They're probably worried sick!"

"My house is not too far from here. Don't you think they would be phoning everybody they knew? Walking and looking for me? Calling the police?" I tried telling different options.

Maria was silent. She then said, "Want a cookie? It's only a dollar."

"No, I'm fine. I'm stuffed. Maria, I will be a regular customer! This is the most delicious pizza I've tasted. *Ever.*"

Maria smiled. "You should go. It's late, and Papa and I are closing."

"Wait, Maria, you said you know my sister?"

"Yeah, she's in my French class. You can ask her if you wish."

"I will. And we're not rich. My dad got demoted from his job. Don't tell Allison I said that."

"I won't tell anyone at all. Waiter's honor." She smiled. Her caramel-colored hair's luster shone brightly in the light.

I got up from my seat, said thank-you to Maria, and pushed open the door. I felt really good. Even better if Mom and Dad noticed.

That was when I realized nothing could be too good.

Chapter 8: No One Notices Leah

When I reached my house, I crept toward the door, and when I went inside, it sounded so quiet, like there was no one there. When I looked in Mom and Dad's room, they were sound asleep. I checked Allison's and Fred's rooms, and surprisingly, they were asleep. Fred usually slept at one. But today, he slept pretty early.

My inside felt like rubber. They didn't even notice.

When I entered my room, Daisy was not sleeping in her blue crib; she was wide awake. She clapped her hands when I entered the room. "Lee," my baby sister squealed. I couldn't even smile. Only my lovely baby sister noticed I was gone.

I marched to my closet. I changed into my striped pajamas. Daisy was still awake. Suddenly, I loved my sister even more than I did before. She put her arms up. "Up!" she cried. I picked her up and took her with me to bed. For the first time, I slept with my little sister.

"I love you, Dandelion Daisy."

I woke up late in the morning since it was a Saturday. Daisy was sleeping, sucking her thumb. I put her back in her crib. I put on my penguin slippers and went in the dining room.

I was very cross with my family.

Mom put a piece of buttered toast on my plate. "Anything bothering you?" she asked absentmindedly.

"No."

Suddenly, I exploded with a question. "Allison, do you know Maria?"

"Umm . . . only one. Maria Cortez. She's in my French class. You'd think a Spanish person would take Spanish instead of French. She's such an ugly nerd."

"*She is not!*" I yelled, banging on the table. "You little brat! Look at your face! Soo much makeup! It's not going to make you look better—"

"Leah Karris! Hold your tongue!" Mom hissed angrily.

"No, I won't! Not anymore!"

Allison spoke up, "You don't even know her, twerp!"

"I do. You probably don't know that, do you, family?" I was talking like a dope. "Do you, family?" Wow, that was just stupid. They were silent.

"You probably don't know this either. I snuck out last night."

Allison and Fred laughed. "You did not!" said Allison, pretending to wipe tears from her eyes.

"*I did too!*"

Dad said sympathetically, like I was retarded and he was trying to calm me down, "Leah, I think we would've noticed if you snuck out."

"Well, you didn't! I went to Pete's Pizzeria. Oh, and, Dad, you better win the lottery because Allison's been spreading lies about us being rich. She also said that Fred has a scholarship to Princeton."

Allison gawked at me. "I didn't—I mean— *How did you know?*"

"I snuck out! That's how. Maria also told me that there was this family, the Karris family, and you didn't even tell about me, the unwanted middle child. Thanks for making me realize that I'm a disgrace."

Silence fell over the kitchen table again.

"I have to go to detention now." I pushed my chair.

I ran to my room and put on my clothes. I didn't even brush my hair.

Chapter 9: Good News

Detention was not that bad. Mr. Crows didn't remark or anything; he just graded papers.

When half an hour was up, I rushed out of the door and rode my bike home.

Everything was very awkward when I entered. I just ran to my room and locked the door. My poster of Harry Potter fell because I slammed the door hard.

Mom and Dad knocked on my door. "Honey, please open the—"

I did. I was not like Allison the brat and drama queen. Okay, maybe I was being a little dramatic, but at least not like Allison! As soon as I opened the door, Mom revealed, "We have good news! We decided to let you go to New York, Leah! Plus, you're going as an unaccompanied minor! Ray is also putting some money in your ticket." Mom was smiling, but you could see the dark circles around her eyes. Dad was on his phone and only looked up when he heard the word *money*.

"Really? Really?" I was so happy! All my troubles of being the unwanted child just went away.

"Uh-huh. You're going for the whole winter break."

"Thanks, Mom! Thanks, Dad!" I rushed to my calendar. Only thirty-four days until I go to the city that never sleeps. Finally. A break from my "loving" family.

Chapter 10: Too Many Butterflies

The day before winter break started, and my stomach was filled with butterflies. Not because of nervousness but because of excitement. I had never met Nelly before, but I had met Eric once when I was three. Uncle Ray came to visit three times, when I was three, six, and eight. I met with Aunt Denise only one time, when I was really little, so I barely remember her. Nelly was my age, and Eric was Fred's age.

In the midst of all this excitement, I noticed Sondra Andreas, Allison's friend, was at home. For some reason, they were in my room, looking in my dresser and drawers. "Mexico's going to be so much fun!" Allison whooped.

Sondra had pale skin and auburn hair. "Yes, Allison! My mom is going to allow us to go to the beach."

Allison raised her eyebrows. Her brown curls, which she had curled this morning, stopped bouncing. "What? I thought your brother, Sander, is going to take us, and he doesn't care what we do."

Sondra shrugged. "Well, Mama thought that it will be best to go with them. It's okay, they're cool."

"No adults are cool after the age of thirty," Allison remarked in a firm voice.

I felt bad for Sondra. My sister was so mean. Who did she think she was? Some kind of queen who could declare that all adults were not cool after the age of thirty?

"Get out of my room, Allison. *Now.*"

"Shut up. I'm looking for my coconut lip gloss I know you took."

"I didn't take any of your lip glosses. I would care less." My voice got louder when she ignored me. *"I said get out!"*

Sondra spoke up, "Let's go, Allison. There is no lip gloss."

Allison rolled her eyes. "Be quiet, Sondra! If she didn't get the lip gloss, who did? Wait a second, at the end of school, Maria Cortez said my lip gloss smelled good. I left my bag for a minute, and I haven't seen my lip gloss since then."

"What are you trying to say?" I asked in an irked tone.

"Maria Cortez took my lip gloss! That sneaky little thief!"

"She didn't! I bet she has better lip glosses than yours!"

Allison marched out of my room, Sondra trotting behind her. What a brat!

Mom called from the kitchen, "Leah, did you pack?"

"Yeah, almost, Mom! Thanks again for letting me go. I'm so darn excited!"

"Ray and Denise and the kids are happy to see you too. Now, pack the rest of your stuff."

Dad came late that evening. He noticed me thirty minutes after he came and only when we sat on the dinner table. Fred was not on the table. He had gone out with his friends. Allison was probably upstairs with Sondra and doing God knows what. I was happy to be alone with Mom and Dad, talking about my trip.

"How's the unaccompanied minor?" Dad chuckled.

"Good! I'm done packing, Dad. Wait, Mom, who'll drop me to the airport? Who'll pick me up from New York airport?"

"Uncle Ray will. We'll drop you. Then when the flight attendant comes, we can leave," Dad informed me.

I had so many butterflies by then I could barely eat.

Chapter 11: New York, Here I Come!

I woke up at five that morning. My flight was at eight. Allison was sound asleep. She was going to Mexico in the evening. Fred was pulling an all-nighter and finishing up a school project that was due the next day. Parents were mad at him because he had a bad habit of doing his work at the very last moment.

"Leah, time to wake up. You're going to New York today," Mom said.

I sat straight up in my bed. Mom handed me some green tea. I sipped it silently. I got dressed into a yellow sweater, which was not a hand-me-down. I brushed my hair. I wanted it to have no knots at all, so I secretly used Allison's straightening iron. I tied my hair into a small ponytail since my hair was short. I put a pink hair band. Perfect. I put on my glasses. I wondered what Nelly looked like.

When I went downstairs, Mom gave me some french toast with powdered sugar. Fred was sleeping while eating his breakfast. He had put his head in his Cheerios. "Fred! Wake up!" Dad said. Startled, Fred woke up, milk dripping from his face. I laughed, and Fred rolled his eyes.

When it was time to go, Fred kind of hugged me. I guess I should call it a pat on the back. Daisy came walking to me and tried grabbing my leg so I wouldn't go.

"I'll be back soon, Daisy!" I said, getting loose of my baby sister's grip. I kissed her cheek. She didn't cry.

When Mom and Dad drove me to the airport, I realized this would be my third time on a plane ride. Once when I was one year old, I went to Paris. I don't remember it at all. Shucks. And I was four or five years old when I went to visit Las Vegas on another plane ride. It was fun.

When we reached the airport, Dad got my luggage out, and Mom got my backpack. We were walking to the check-in when out of the blue, Mom said, "Leah, I hope you don't think that you're a disgrace or the unwanted child. That's not true. Right, Steve?"

"Uh, yeah," Dad said absentmindedly. He was probably thinking about work. I'm pretty sure he wanted to be at work instead of dropping me off.

"I guess so, Mom. And I didn't mean to be rude to you guys or anything."

"I know, Leah. Just please don't do it again."

I wasn't really sure about that but I was pretty sure without me in the family, it would probably be exactly the same. Suddenly, I thought that I wasn't a disgrace or unwanted. Out of so many children, I was just an extra.

Before I knew it, I was done with check-in. Then security. Now it was time for me to board my flight. I had to wear a Unaccompanied Minor (UM) card on my neck. Mom and Dad had an escort pass so they could go to security check-in with me.

Alice, a flight attendant, was there and welcomed me with a broad smile. "Hi, are you Leah?"

"Err . . . yes."

"I'm Alice. Nice to meet you, Leah." Then she turned to Mom and Dad.

"I'll take it from here, Mr. and Mrs. Karris." Mom and Dad hugged me and said good-bye.

"Bye, Mom, bye, Dad."

Another flight attendant got my suitcase and escorted me to my seat. I sat down. I got a window seat. Alice came again. "It's time to take off!"

"Oh. Cool."

"Well, dear, put on your seat belt, and I'll be checking on you."

"Okay, Alice." I strapped myself in with the dark-blue seat belt and felt excited sitting without an adult by my side.

I looked at the window. The plane was in line to take off. I was jittery. Finally, the plane went up. I got my backpack and started to write in my journal I got a long time ago but never wrote in or touched, so it was in very good shape.

Dear Journal,

The plane just took off. Can't wait for New York! I wonder if Nelly has short hair like me or long hair. I wonder what her hair color is. Maybe she hates crafts like me and can't cut well . . . I'm honestly more of a good writer than an artist.

—Leah

After a while, Alice came again and asked me
if I wanted a drink. I wanted a soda with light ice.
I also got complimentary salted peanuts. I doodled
on my journal for a bit and read *Harry Potter and
the Order of the Phoenix*. But the plane ride was
boring, and I longed to reach New York already.

I had a million questions about Uncle Ray, Nelly, Eric, and Aunt Denise. What kind of house did they have? Was Nelly allergic to pumpkin seeds like me?

Finally, after about five hours, forty-three minutes, and a bad headache, I reached New York City. "We have now reached New York City. The temperature is thirty-three degrees outside. Hope you enjoyed flying on Evolvo Airlines," announced the pilot. I looked at my yellow sweater. It surely didn't look suitable for the weather.

Alice and I walked with my luggage. I spotted Uncle Ray with his black hair and blue eyes, unlike my mother, who had brown eyes like me, from the escalator. He was wearing khakis and a sweater. A girl who had wavy black hair with sea-blue eyes said to Uncle Ray, "When will she get here?" She seemed very impatient. And very pink. She was wearing a pink sweater with pink earrings and a blue-and-pink vest with pink leggings and sparkly white boots. She held an—oh my god—iPhone! It had a—ugh—pink cover with cute koalas on it.

Obviously, she was Nelly. That made me feel forlorn. I didn't want my first cousin to be impatient and, well, pink.

"Oh, she's here!" Uncle Ray exclaimed.

I waved. "Hi, Uncle Ray. Hi, Nelly."

Before both of them could answer, Alice interrupted. "Please sign this form, Mr.—" She didn't sound so sweetie-sweet like when she was in the plane ride.

"Braces. And this is my beautiful niece, Leah Karris." Wow, my mom's maiden name was weird. But it's not like a last name like Karris is normal.

I blushed ruby red.

After signing some forms, we went outside, and I'm pretty sure I *tasted* hypothermia. When Uncle Ray saw me almost freezing to death, he shouted to Nelly, "Nelly! Go get the jacket we brought for Leah!"

Nelly quickly came close to me. I realized how nice and pretty she looked even if she looked like a pink blob. Her hair smelled like strawberries. "Here," she said, handing me a fluffy jacket. I saw Nelly and Uncle Ray only wearing light jackets. How did they deal with the gruesome cold like that? On the car ride, Nelly put on some music on her iPhone. "New Yorkers can deal with the coldest temperatures!"

When we arrived, my jaw dropped. They lived in a forty-seven-story apartment! "Let's go, Leah!" said Nelly, grabbing my hand.

Chapter 12: Apartment 2345

When we entered apartment 2345, I first saw a big glass window that showed an outstanding view of New York. There was an upstairs level too.

"Okay, girls, Eric's coming from his computer club soon, and Aunt Denise is coming from the hospital at eight," Uncle Ray said. Aunt Denise was a pediatrician. "Nelly, can you make the dinner?"

How could Nelly make dinner? I thought. *She must be one of those who* pretend *to be mature and responsible types.*

"Sure, Dad. Come on, Leah! Help me cook."

We entered the kitchen, which had a nice fragrance. Nelly first got some tomato sauce and cut some peppers. Then she put the tomato sauce in the saucer and put butter inside. She put the peppers in and spaghetti noodles.

Nelly tossed a salad with dressing and croutons. After that, she mashed the potatoes, which were already boiled in a ceramic bowl, and added some salt and butter.

"Wow, Nelly, that's really cool! I can't cook anything but cereal and toast."

Nelly laughed. "It just takes practice, and I enjoy it." Maybe I kind of misjudged Nelly.

Nelly added some black pepper to the buttery mashed potatoes. "Leah, can you get out the salmon?" she asked.

"Okay." I got out the salmon, and Nelly asked some help from Uncle Ray to help fry it in the frying pan.

"All right, now get out of the kitchen. I'm cooking a surprise dessert!"

I went out of the kitchen. I wondered what to do, since Uncle Ray was attending to an important phone call and Nelly was not letting me inside the kitchen. I decided to go upstairs. There were five rooms. I wanted to go to Nelly's room first. I entered inside the door that had a sign that said Nelly's Room.

The walls were painted light blue with pink paper hearts, and in the middle was a bed with a bedding of pink-and-saffron sheets. There were about twenty stuffed animals in here. I heard a door open. Eric must've come.

"I can't believe that I'm not picked to go to the finals in Los Angeles!" he said as he put his bag down. Just like Uncle Ray, he had black hair, but he had black eyes. "Dad? Nelly?"

Nelly came out of the kitchen. She was wearing an apron now, and it was a mess. "Leah arrived," she said anxiously and went back to the kitchen.

"Oh, hi, Leah, welcome to New York!"

"Hi, Eric!"

"Um . . . was the plane ride comfortable?" he asked a corny question. I missed my brother, Fred, just for a second, as Eric seemed to be a mature version of him.

"Yeah."

"Oh, good. Have you seen Dad?"

"Um . . . I think he's upstairs."

After a while, Aunt Denise came. She was beautiful. Aunt Denise had wavy brown hair to her neck. Unlike mine, it wasn't ugly brown. She had black eyes, which were stunning and like Eric's. She was still wearing her doctor uniform.

"Hi, kids! And, Leah!" Aunt Denise had a British accent, which sounded lovely.

"I'm so glad to have you here!" she hugged me. I immediately loved her.

"I'm so glad to *be* here!"

By then I knew I would have the time of my life here in New York. And this visit, I thought later on, changed my life.

Chapter 13: Nelly's Fabulous Dinner

Nelly set the table for dinner. "Okay, my specialty tonight! Salad, mashed potatoes, spaghetti, and salmon. And . . ." She presented a dish that made everyone's mouth water. Chocolate molten lava cake!

"My goodness, Nelly, you're an excellent cook!" Aunt Denise exclaimed.

"Yeah, Nel, you actually have a talent for cooking. The only thing you can do," Eric said. Nelly playfully stuck her tongue out at Eric.

Uncle Ray just looked like he wanted to eat as soon as possible.

"Bon appétit!" Nelly said.

I put a bit of everything on my plate except the cake; I would eat that after I chatted with my relatives.

"So, Leah, how's school?" asked Aunt Denise as she put paprika on her spaghetti.

"Good, except I have mean teachers."

"Really? Who?" Uncle Ray said, his mouth full.

"Mrs. Lean and Mrs. Albright."

"Aunt Denise, where did you grow up?" I spoke in a very sophisticated voice to impress her.

"Oh, I grew up in Birmingham, England."

I finally tried a bit of the spaghetti. "Oh. My. God. Nelly, this is amazing!"

Nelly blushed. "Thanks."

Uncle Ray then said, "Leah, you excited for the ball drop?"

"Oh, yes! It's going to be absolutely amazing, right, Nelly?"

"I've never been to it. We live far from there. I usually watch it on TV."

"Tomorrow, let's take Leah to Niagara Falls," Eric stated. Well, he was different from my brother because he actually ate dinner with his family!

"Sure, let's do that!" Uncle Ray exclaimed.

Chapter 14: Aunt Denise's Plans

In the next couple of days, I went to a lot of places in New York. Niagara Falls, Central Park, the Empire State Building, Statue of Liberty, and Ground Zero. All this time, Nelly, Eric, Aunt Denise, and Uncle Ray had fun. I did too. But after three days of enjoyment, tears burned in the back of my eyes. My family never had fun together like this. I didn't know what to do. I wished that I could stay here in New York forever.

Aunt Denise came inside the guest bedroom I was staying in.

"Leah, are you all right?" she asked. My aunt seemed like she could read minds.

"Yes," I said, blinking back my tears.

"Anything wrong?"

"No."

She smiled warmly. "Tell me, dear."

I couldn't help myself. I sobbed and sobbed away. Thank goodness Nelly, Eric, and Uncle Ray had gone to the store.

"Ever since Fred started high school and Allison started junior high and Daisy was born, all my family hates one another. All they do is fight, and they don't care or pay attention. The other time, I sneaked out, they didn't even notice. You guys are the example of a perfect family. We never have fun anymore, even if I try!" I burst into tears again. "I can't take it anymore, Aunt Denise, I really can't!"

Aunt Denise looked sympathetic and worried. "That must be so hard on you, Leah. You should tell your parents. And just because it doesn't look like it, they all love one another."

"Mom and Dad are too busy, and I don't know if they love each other or not! They all fight so much." Then I told her about my running-away experiment.

"Sweetheart, your family loves you a lot. It seems tough, but you'll get over it. Things are probably changing. Also, I'm sure they forgot after a busy day." She squeezed my hand.

"Change can be a good or bad thing. So far, it's bad! I want life back to how it used to be when I was younger and they cared."

"Leah, you are the bravest girl I ever met."

"Me? How?"

"You act like you don't care, but you do. You try to make your family talk and have fun. You never cry unless your feelings burst out, which is rare."

"How do you know?"

Aunt Denise smiled again. "I can tell."

"Aunt Denise, I'm sick of it."

"It all starts with you, Leah."

"How?"

"Make a change yourself. Try, try, and try."

"I don't want to!"

"Yes, you do. Don't lie, dear. Spend more time with your siblings even if they don't want to. First, compliment them and—"

I stared at her and blinked. "You don't know what I'm going through, being the middle child," I said gently. I didn't want to sound like I was being rude or disrespectful.

"Yes, I do. I was the middle child. My mom and my brother fought. My younger sister was kind of bratty. I felt exactly the same way you do right now. Do you know how I got over it?"

I shrugged per habit and hunched my shoulders so much that they started to hurt.

"I tried changing my family. I did an FYF, a family yelling flip chart. Don't tell your parents and record how many times someone yells at one another. If it is over six, inform your siblings and parents. They will realize and try to stop. But, sweetie, you have to realize—"

I didn't let her complete her sentence and jumped up and hugged Aunt Denise. "You're the best!" The moment I reached home, I would do this FYF. I didn't even think about what Aunt Denise said about realizing. But I knew, in a way, she wanted me to learn it myself.

Chapter 15: Mrs. Evilright

Nelly came home from the store. She looked happy.

"Jelly is back home!" She carried a puppy with golden-whitish fur.

"You have a puppy?" I asked with amazement.

"Yes! He was at Ob's Obedience School. Isn't he fantastic?"

Aunt Denise looked at Jelly. "Are you sure he's trained?" she asked. "When we first got him, he peed everywhere!"

"Yes, I'm sure!"

Uncle Ray caught my eye. "Leah, why are your eyes red and puffy?"

Aunt Denise answered for me, "She's tired, Ray. Time change, of course." Then she winked at me.

I grinned. My aunt was awesome.

Uncle Ray spoke up, "The Patterson family is coming for dinner."

"Yay!" Nelly exclaimed.

"Who's the Patterson family?" I asked.

"Donald Patterson, a close colleague of mine in college, and his family. He lives on twenty-eighth floor of this building. He came back with his family from Europe yesterday." Uncle Ray peeked at his watch.

Eric spoke up, "My best friend is Tom Patterson."

"Hannah Patterson is my best friend!" Nelly said happily. "You'll just love her, Leah, I know!" She jumped around, her puppy trotting behind her.

Aunt Denise didn't look pleased.

Uncle Ray went upstairs to his room. Nelly and I put one last ornament on the Christmas tree and headed to her room to play Monopoly.

While I set the board, Nelly looked inside my beaded purse. She read my notebook when I wasn't looking and started reading it out loud.

The Girl and the Evil Teacher

By Leah Mary Karris

Once, a young girl lived in a ~~manchin~~ ~~masion~~ ~~mansin~~ house by the ocean. One day, it was time for the first day of school. All her teachers were nice so far, and they liked her.

When she reached her school, her teacher was writing rules on the ~~bord~~ board. She had yellow teeth and green skin! She was a witch! Her name was Mrs. ~~Albright~~ Evilright. Mrs. Evilright looked at the girl. "Ah, hello, ~~Leah~~ girl. Take a seat."

A strong wind blew, and the door was open on purpose, so the kids got sick, and a big ax flew in! Of course, the girl screamed. Wouldn't you?

"Girl! Go sit outside!"

"But, Mrs. Evilright—"

"No buts! Get out of this classroom immediately!"

The poor girl almost froze to death. She was mad.

A ~~foolis~~ foolish girl came outside. *"Come inside! You will be punished!"*

"What did I do?" asked the girl.

"Mrs. Evilright!" The foolish girl ran back in.

The girl sat and sneezed.

"So you like to be rude, ay?" Mrs. Evilright said with a sneer.

"I didn't do anything, Mrs. Evilright."

"Yes, you did! Go to Mr. ~~Holcomb~~ Hobart's office now!"

The girl got detention for the rest of her life until she graduated college.

The End

This story is based on real-life events. If you would like to arest these people, please talk to Leah Mary Karris, 821 Pablo Court, Cherry City, California.

Nelly laughed and laughed. "Leah, this is great!"

"Um, thanks."

"Oh, *mansion* is spelled M-A-N-S-I-O-N. And *arrest* is spelled A-R-R-E-S-T."

A doorbell rang. "Hannah!" Nelly squealed.

She raced down the stairs, and I went slowly behind her.

Chapter 16: Nelly and Hannah: The Bullies

A girl with curly sunny-blond hair and blue-green eyes came, chewing gum. She did not smile until she saw Nelly. Hannah Patterson was wearing a shirt that said Diva Girl, and it was red with black sparkles. She was wearing dangling earrings that jingled and had a purse with an iPhone, just like Nelly.

Meanwhile, Eric greeted Tom, and Uncle Ray talked to Mr. Patterson. Mrs. Patterson and Aunt Denise were giving each other artificial smiles. Mrs. Patterson was wearing a red overcoat and lots of ruby lipstick. Her blond hair was tied up in a high bun with a silver bow stuck on it.

"Hi, Denise," Mrs. Patterson said without showing even the slightest courtesy in her voice.

"Hello, Lola," Aunt Denise replied, refusing to smile. "How marvelous you look today!"

Mrs. Patterson did another fake smile. "Oh, thank you. May I say, Denise, you look quite nice yourself."

After Nelly and her friend hugged, Hannah stared at me. She turned to Nelly. "Who's this?" the so far rude girl demanded.

"Oh, this is Leah Karris. She's my cousin."

Uncle Ray spoke up, "Please welcome my dear niece Leah Karris, Donald, Lola, Tom, and Hannah."

Each person in the Patterson family said hi to me except Hannah.

After a while, Hannah continued chewing her gum. Finally, she said, "What kind of a name is Leah Karris, anyways?"

I was outraged. I was about to say, *"What kind of a name is Hannah Patterson, anyways?"* But Aunt Denise called us for bread and olive oil and vinegar.

The combination of olive oil and vinegar was tasty with the sour dough bread. Everything was going okay until a knock on the door came.

"That must be Johnny." Uncle Ray pushed his chair to answer the door.

"Johnny, coming in for dinner?" my uncle questioned.

"Of course, Ray!" Aunt Denise said in a tender tone.

A lady and a man stood in the doorway. A little girl was standing a few feet beside them. She had black pigtails with ribbons and a big yellow dress, which was smeared with dirt. She was very chubby and short. I couldn't exactly see her eyes at first because bangs covered her face until her nose.

I heard Hannah say, "Ooh, it's the Johnsons! The family that are janitors for our apartment! They live on the ugly first floor."

Nelly slightly giggled.

I didn't.

Johnny Johnson said, "Minnie, go talk to them." He pointed to Nelly, Hannah, and me.

Minnie came to us. "Hello," she said very quietly.

Hannah said something to Nelly, then she went to Uncle Ray and whispered, "Dad, they're janitors!"

"So?" he said snappishly.

"They shouldn't join us for our graceful meal, they should wash the dishes!"

"Nelly Braces, behave yourself or I'll put the gracefulness in this meal out of here!" he whisper-yelled. Nelly scowled and went back to her seat.

I wanted to be polite to Minnie, so I asked, "How old are you, Minnie?"

"Nine." Wow, she was puny for her age! She looked up, and I saw her eyes. They were sparkly blue but different from Nelly's. They were light blue, and Nelly's had a very dense shade of blue. To me, they were pretty.

"What's your name?" Minnie looked around the apartment.

"Leah."

"That's nice." But then she was silent as a snail for a long while.

Uncle Ray chatted with Mr. Patterson and Mr. Johnson. "Hey, girls, why don't you play in Nelly's room until dinner?"

We headed upstairs. Nelly and Hannah, arm to arm, smirked while they walked and exchanged secrets. They looked at Minnie a lot.

"Let's play family," Hannah said. I knew something was up from her tone. "I'll be the mom, Nelly will be the big sister, and Leah will be the dad."

Nelly said sarcastically, "Hannah, oh no, there's no more parts for wittle Minnie!"

It's little *and not* wittle, I thought in my head. *What sort of words people say to mock others.*

"Are you stupid, Nel?"

"Right, she can be the baby. To be precise, a dumb, idiot baby." But every time she said something mean, Nelly just looked regretful afterward.

"Nope, she's way too ugly and *fat*. How about . . . maid? Servant? Or *janitor*? Just like her poor parents. After all, she weighs about a hundred pounds."

"True, true!"

Minnie looked hurt. Her eyes swam with tears. This was too much for me.

"That's mean, Hannah! Even you, Nelly! I expected better from you!"

Nelly started to have this guilty look on her face, but Hannah interrupted.

"Nobody asked you. Mind your own business, okay? You're not our mother."

Eric entered a moment later. "Dinner's ready!"

Hannah and Nelly left. I stayed behind with Minnie. "I'm sorry about them," I said to her.

"It's okay, I'm used to it. At school, they tease me at recess." I felt bad for her. I decided to confront Nelly, and if she and Hannah didn't apologize, I would tell Uncle Ray or Aunt Denise.

Chapter 17: Bratty Nelly

When every guest was gone, I went to Nelly's room. She was on her iPhone, texting Hannah.

"Nelly, a word?" I stood outside her door.

"Okay, come in."

Nelly was in her cute doggy pajamas. Her hair was tied in a loose braid. Jelly was sleeping right beside her.

"Nelly, I don't know how to say this politely, but you're being a bully. Um, never mind what I said. I just meant—"

She gawked at me. "I'm not being a bully, Leah." Her tone was firm.

"You do act mean to Minnie Johnson. Teasing is bullying."

Nelly raised her eyebrows. "I do not. Can't she take a joke? Can't *you*?"

"Of course I can, but I don't think Minnie likes it. I certainly won't. Your friend Hannah is the one who made you like this. Minnie told me that you pick on her in school."

"Hannah did not do anything, Leah." Her tone got meaner.

I was sick of being polite. "Nelly, if you want to continue being a bully, go ahead. I just think you're being mean." I turned to leave.

"Leah, if you want to act like this, leave *my* house."

I faced her and looked straight in her eyes. "Excuse me?"

"Yes, I said that. Have a problem with that?"

I was angry. I didn't know why I did it or what I was trying to do, I just muttered "Brat" and wrote it on Nelly's hand with a Sharpie. She tried squiggling away from my firm grip, but she couldn't.

"What did you do?" she shrieked. "*I am not a brat, you are!*"

"Says the person who has an iPhone and who has twenty stuffed animals and *silk* robes!"

Nelly's face got as red as a beetroot.

"Get out of my room!"

I marched out of Nelly's room. I wasn't sure, but I think I heard sobbing as I slammed her door.

Uncle Ray and Aunt Denise had gone to get a phone fixed. Eric, in his skull T-shirt and dark-blue pajamas, came walking into the hallway.

"What's going on here?" he asked.

Before I could answer, Nelly came out of her room. "Mind your own business, Eric!" That was the first time I noticed Nelly talking to Eric this way.

Eric raised his eyebrows. "I don't have time for this, Nelly Braces. I'm going, but if I hear any more yelling—and I'm trying to focus and concentrate on test practice—I'll tell Dad—"

"Go on, be a tattletale," Nelly snapped.

"Nel, go ahead and be a brat. I don't care. Just *stop* yelling."

"*I am not a brat!*" This time, she burst into tears even harder.

Eric looked at me then Nelly and went to her. "Calm down. I was joking."

Nelly pointed to me. "She's . . . not . . . joking!"

Eric just sighed. "Just sort it out yourselves. I have to study." He walked away, his black eyes frowning. "And by the way, Leah, she's a little bit of a drama queen," he whispered. "Good luck with her."

Nelly didn't speak to me and went to her room. I heard familiar music. I couldn't help myself. It had been ages since I heard it because I never got to use the computer.

"Emma Donatello?"

Nelly turned and faced me. "Yes, and what do you want?"

"Nelly, I'm sorry, okay? I didn't mean to hurt you. I just felt you were rude to Minnie."

"Am I a brat?" She literally asked that question.

"No, but you act like one. I know you're not actually like that, but other people don't know how nice and kind you are. Hannah will turn you into a brat *and* a bully."

"What's wrong with Hannah?"

"She's a bully, Nelly, and it's true." Nelly just sat there.

"I'll tell her to stop. I felt bad for Minnie at first when Hannah started calling her Minnie Mouse Janitor, but Hannah told me not to since it was just a joke."

"A joke that can hurt somebody. Just like when Eric said you were a brat. Joking and bullying are different. Trust me, I know."

"How do you know?"

I tried changing the subject. "I love Emma Donatello. She's amazing and beautiful."

"Me too! I have lots of posters of her, but I don't know how I can hang them on the wall if it is already full of pictures of me, cute pink butterflies and hearts, a purple clock, and—"

"Don't worry. I know what to do." Nelly and I started taking out some of the butterflies and hearts by using a mini ladder. I was very good at it, but Nelly wasn't getting the hang of it. I removed one picture of Nelly when she visited Disneyland. Then I placed one poster of Emma Donatello playing piano. Emma's red hair sparkled from the sunrays.

"That looks nice," Nelly said.

"Thanks. Now give me that other poster." We—mostly I—placed three more posters on the wall. When I saw her stuffed animal collection, I asked her if I could redecorate it.

"Why?" Nelly asked.

"It'll look nice. I promise." Nelly went out of the room.

I put most of the stuffed animals in her gigantic closet. I looked at the edge of her wardrobe, and I found some good stuff. I spotted an old landline phone with a gold crust and fuzzy green edges.

"Perfect!" I exclaimed. I put that on her bedside table. It might not work, but it looked very good. I moved the desk where it overlooked the view from her window. I put all her schoolbooks on one side of the desk and put her electronics on the other.

I changed her pink bedding. I needed to look for some-other-colored bedding. Her room can't look all pink-y. It just looked bad. I couldn't find anything in her closet, so I quietly went into Uncle Ray and Aunt Denise's room. I found a very pretty multicolored bedding. It had one square that was pink with blue ruffles, one that was green, the other had yellow and blue dots, and one that was blue with gray squares. I made her bed and put three stuffed animals on it. I found some paint, and I just had to do something.

I painted a picture of a butterfly on her blue wall. It was really pretty, with pink wings, and the middle part of the butterfly was yellow, and it was smiling. Her wall now did not look very crowded. The only things I put on the bedside table were the phone and a couple of books.

After I redecorated her room, I was worried. I should've asked Nelly if it was okay to do it. I suspected Nelly was outside somewhere because obviously she should've checked on what I was doing. I checked the time on Nelly's purple clock, and three hours had passed. I crept into Eric's room, and he was taking a nap.

Chapter 18: I Should've Asked

The minute Nelly saw her newly redecorated room, she stood frozen.

"Leah!" she cried. "This . . . is . . . just . . . amazing!"

"Really, do you like it?"

"Yep, it's awesome!"

"I'm glad you like it."

The next day, I got ready, and Uncle Ray, Aunt Denise, and Eric sat on the kitchen table. After a while, Nelly came down.

"Hey, Nel, can you warm the french toast?" Eric spoke.

"No, I don't feel like it. I'm going downstairs. Hannah's there."

"Nelly?" Aunt Denise said sharply before Nelly could go out of the door.

"Yeah, Mom?"

"Have you studied for the math test that is coming after winter break?"

"Um . . . well . . . yes . . . no."

"Go study, then you may go."

"But, Mom—"

"No buts. Go study."

"Dad! Tell Mom—"

"No, Nelly, your mother's right. Go study!" Uncle Ray's tone was stern.

Nelly stomped her feet and went back into her room.

"Leah, Minnie asked if you could meet her down in the lobby," Uncle Ray said.

"Okay, um, now?"

"Uh, yeah. I can tell Johnny—"

"No, no, I'll go. Let me just wear my jacket and boots." I did that and went to the lobby.

I spotted Minnie wearing a jacket and torn earmuffs. "Hi, Leah, do you want to go outside in the park near the apartment?"

"Okay, but isn't it snowing?"

"It's not snowing, but the park has a little bit of snow on it. It's all right, though, let's go!"

Hannah was there. I frowned.

"Hi, Little Miss Minnie Mouse Janitor! And, Leah, the girl who pokes in other people's business. Where's Nelly?"

"Oh, can it Hannah. Nobody cares about your mean remarks except yourself."

"Yeah!" squeaked Minnie. Hannah raised her eyebrows, and Nelly came in the nick of time.

"Hey, Hannah!" Nelly said. Her hair was down, and she was wearing a gray sweatshirt.

"Hi, Nelly! *What are you wearing?*"

"Oh, it's my brother's old sweatshirt."

"Well, it's *disgusting!*"

I snapped at Hannah, "Have you seen your clothes? It looks like a rainbow puked on you."

Hannah snorted. "Shut up. You're ugly—"

"Look at yourself in the mirror. It looks like you graduated from Clown College," I replied rudely.

Nelly said, "Guys, can we just stop insulting one another?"

"Fine. Let's hang out in your house." Hannah turned away and flipped her long hair, hitting my face.

Minnie looked frightened by Hannah.

"Um, Minnie, are you coming?"

"No, I'm going home." I could barely hear her voice.

Nelly and Hannah were already in the new room.

"What happened to your room? It looks H-E-D-O-U-S! Hideous!"

"Actually, *hideous* is spelled H-I-D-E-O-U-S," Nelly said.

"Don't correct me!" she shrieked. Aunt Denise came in the room. She looked as if she were about to interrogate, but her eyes landed on the butterfly. I chewed on my fingernails.

I knew I should've asked!

Chapter 19: The Last of Hannah Patterson's Bullying

It turned out Aunt Denise thought the painted butterfly was cute.

At first she said, "Nelly Braces, you know you're not supposed to paint on walls. That's a three-year-old thing to do. But I must say that it is very pretty."

"I didn't do it, Mom. It was Leah," Nelly replied.

Aunt Denise turned to face me. "Err, Leah, did you—"

"Redecorate this room? Yes, and I'm sorry for doing it, Aunt Denise. I should've asked first. I'm very sorry."

Aunt Denise's face turned softer. "It's all right, sweetie. It's very cute, but just ask next time, okay?

As for you, Hannah, I suggest you go. Nelly has to study."

Nelly looked like she was about to argue, and Hannah whispered something in her ear. Nelly looked angry.

Aunt Denise examined the new room. "I remember this landline phone! I got it when I first came to the USA from England. It's so pretty! The bedding, oh, I got this for Eric when he was younger, but he thought it was a girl thing. I just didn't have the heart to throw this lovely thing out—"

Hannah interjected, "Mrs. Braces, that's nice and all, but let us have our time to play now ! Nelly wants to play with me and she can study later. And also, you can't *boss* me, Nelly, or anybody—"

Aunt Denise was shocked and before she could say anything, Nelly shouted, *"Enough. That is enough!"* The words came out of Nelly's mouth faster than a roadrunner trying to catch its prey. She was fuming.

"Leah was right! You're being rude and you're mean to Minnie and my family. *Do not dare talk to my family that way, understood?* I am never going to be mean to Minnie again. I'm acting like a brat and bully, just like you! It has to stop, I mean it!"

Hannah had raised her eyebrows, and her face scrunched up, and it turned red, as if she were about to cry!

She ran out of Nelly's room and closed the door loud. Hannah was gone by the time we reached the living room.

Hurray! Hannah won't be a bully now for sure.

But why did Nelly look so sad?

Chapter 20: Nelly's Punishment

"I have no idea what just happened," Aunt Denise stated while walking out of Nelly's room. "I couldn't understand Hannah's voice. It sounded so . . .offensive, teenager-like."

"I stood up to a rude and mean girl. She deserved it," Nelly said, but she was still frowning.

Aunt Denise got a ginger drink and poured it into three glasses. "Let's talk about it, shall we?"

Nelly took a deep breath. "When I started school this year, fifth grade, Hannah and I were great friends. She's always been a little candid and bossy, but this year it just got worse. I didn't want to lose her as a friend, so I made fun of tons of people, just like Hannah did. We also gossiped about people, and we passed notes to them saying mean things. Some of the times it was my idea! Not just Hannah's! And I feel terrible. Yesterday, Hannah picked on Minnie Johnson. I did too, and I feel even *more* terrible. Why did I do it? I don't know myself. I'm such a bad person! I had enough today, the way she talked about you and Leah. I'm done with her— forever. I don't want to be a bully."

Aunt Denise seemed mad at Nelly. "I'm glad you told me. It's not like you're going off the hook on this. Bullying is a real issue, and it's not fun. And also, Hannah isn't a real friend if she wants you to do bad stuff."

I gulped down the rest of my drink. I mumbled, "Bullying is horrible . . . I know. One time, Zoe Hawk gossiped about me all around the school, and after gym class, she put my shoes in the trash. I still feel miserable about it."

Aunt Denise nodded and started a long talk with Nelly. "I'm talking to your principal about you and Hannah and bullying in general. You have already told me, that's good, and I am happy that you understood sooner. But we need to let every student know that it isn't okay. And, Nelly, your phone will be taken from you, and no more meeting friends for the rest of winter break. No TV, computer, iPad, or any other electronic. The only place you can go to is the ball drop. I was stupid to give you a phone at the age of eleven, so you might not even get it back. You text too much. Missy, you've got to start doing better things and, yes, getting a bit more serious about your school. You failed on your math test last month. Consider yourself grounded, Nelly Marsha Braces."

"I know, I deserve it," Nelly murmured.

Chapter 21: Christmas Day

Days flew by fast in New York, and Christmas Day came in a flash. I couldn't sleep the night before Christmas; I kept tossing and turning and woke up early in the morning.

We had a nice Christmas breakfast: pancakes made by Aunt Denise, eggs made by Nelly, bacon made by Eric (they were pre-ready), hash browns made by Uncle Ray (they were a frozen, microwavable type of food), and I set the table and put the orange juice in glasses since I couldn't cook, or have access to frozen foods.

There were a lot of presents under the Christmas tree. Nelly and Eric opened their gifts immediately, but I lolled around. In the airport gift shop, I got a mini-Theodore from Alvin and the Chipmunks for Nelly, a big pencil box for Eric, a hat for Uncle Ray, and a plastic necklace for Aunt Denise. They were all . . . cheap. Well, I tried.

"Leah, aren't you going to open yours?" Uncle Ray pointed to a stack at the edge of the Christmas tree.

"Err, okay." I felt shy. A phone call came from Mom and Dad to wish me a merry Christmas. Mom and Dad didn't call a lot of times; I guess they were too busy. They said my Christmas present from them was this trip. Well, no complaints there.

I opened my presents. I got a lovely black dress with a pink ribbon from Nelly, a cool electronic dictionary from Eric, a fun box of art projects and paint from Uncle Ray, and a beautiful pair of magenta sandals from Aunt Denise. It made my presents look bad. I felt guilty for giving such cheap gifts.

"Leah, come here," Aunt Denise said. I followed her into her room.

"This is a book for you." My aunt gazed at my confused-looking face.

She handed me a torn old velvet book. The front cover said the following:

Family Forever

(Not in My World)

It was handwritten. "This is really nice, Aunt Denise. Who's the author?"

"I don't know."

"Um . . . where did you get it from?"

"In London. It was a rainy day, and I was trying to find a roof to cover my head, and I found this book."

I didn't know if it was exactly true. Maybe it was.

Aunt Denise turned to leave.

"Aunt Denise, um . . ."

"Yes, dear?"

"Thanks for the lovely gifts from all of you. But I gave horrible gifts to you," I said this very quickly.

"Leah! Don't you dare say anything like this again. We all love the gifts. Sweetie, it's not the gifts but the thought that counts. And by the way, the necklace is so trendy."

I laughed. "Thanks, Aunt Denise."

Uncle Ray announced that the Pattersons were coming for dinner.

"What?" shrieked Nelly. She looked dumbfounded.

"Nelly, what do you mean? We always have dinner with the Pattersons on Christmas," Uncle Ray replied.

"I don't want to have dinner with them. Let's do something fun and by *ourselves* for once. It's always with the Pattersons!" Nelly said.

Uncle Ray looked confused. "Don't you want to meet Hannah?"

Eric got up. "Tom texted me that Hannah was crying and kept saying 'Nelly Braces is the meanest person ever!' over and over."

Uncle Ray's face suddenly became very stern. "What did you do, Nelly? I know you were saying something about the Johnsons the other day, but what about Hannah and the Pattersons?"

Nelly looked at her toes. "Well, um—"

Uncle Ray seemed angry. "You misbehaved, didn't you? Go to your room right now, young lady!"

I guess Aunt Denise didn't tell Uncle Ray about the "incident."

"She didn't do anything, Uncle Ray." I looked at Uncle Ray then Nelly, who was now looking closely at her lap. "Hannah was the bully who made Nelly say and do mean stuff. Finally, she realized it and confronted Hannah. I think it takes guts to stand up to your own best friend who's a bully and . . . well, stop being a bully."

Nelly's face turned pink. She blushed.

Aunt Denise spoke up, "Leah's right, Ray. This is what happened, I witnessed it. Nelly told me she picked on kids at school too. So I'm going to talk to her principal about bullying in general and Nelly and Hannah being the trouble makers. I grounded her with no electronics or meeting friends or going anywhere except the ball drop as a punishment."

Uncle Ray sighed. "I'm going to talk to Donald about this. Until then, I guess we could just go out for dinner." We all went in our rooms.

I decided to read the book that Aunt Denise got me. I flipped to the first page.

September 21, 1985

My dream was to have a family. A perfect family that noticed me.

But they didn't notice me!

I knew what I had to do. Break my arm!

They would give me attention. Loads. Maybe?

So I went to the window, opened it, and jumped out. I would definitely break something.

But I landed on an old mattress my mother kept outside.

Rats!

So I went to the kitchen and put water everywhere. I was about to try to slip, but my mother called me in for doing my chores. I grumbled. I completely forgot about the water in the kitchen. My father came in to get a cup of tea and slipped! Oh, he was mad. I blamed it on my older brother, Charlie.

I don't think I'm going to do any shenanigans anymore.

~Some Person (call me SP)

The book was weird. I mean, who is SP? And is SP a boy or a girl? I'm guessing a girl. See, I mean, only a girl would try to get attention. Maybe I'm wrong.

For dinner, we went to an Italian restaurant. I had chicken pasta with Alfredo sauce. We ate a

Christmas cake with green and red frosting. When we were walking to our car, it got very cold. The wind started to shriek, and snow started to come down rapidly.

"Let's go, now!" Uncle Ray yelled over all that noise. "The roads will be blocked soon!"

I felt a bit worried. We got in the car, and Uncle Ray was right. Soon the roads were filled with several inches of pure white snow.

"Oh no," Aunt Denise said.

"I suppose we have to stay in the car for a while," my uncle stated.

Uncle Ray put the heating on maximum and Christmas songs on the radio so loud that we could barely hear the wind, but when we put off the radio, we could hear the wind screaming.

Nelly's face turned green. "Mom, Dad? I don't feel good. I'm never eating shrimp lasagna ever again." Then she started gagging.

Aunt Denise said, "The snow's dying down. Ray called the snowplow guys, and they're coming soon. Don't worry, sweetie, we're going home soon."

Suddenly, I had a big headache. I was used to the pleasant weather of California, but this sort of weather, no.

It seemed like hours, but the snowplow guys finally came. It took thirty minutes, but then we were on the road back home. Everything was pretty smooth.

But when we arrived, Nelly vomited on the doorstep.

Chapter 22: Deciding What to Wear

"We need to decide what we're going to wear for the ball drop, Leah!" Nelly exclaimed three days before New Year's Day.

"Nelly, you know the ball drop's in three days, right?"

"So? We're late to decide what outfit we're going to wear!"

I winced. I hated clothes and shopping.

When Nelly saw my bag, she looked like she ate something sour. "No dresses? Or skirts?"

I shrugged, wanting to say, "What's the big deal?"

"That's it. You're going to have to wear some of my clothes." My cousin grabbed my hand, and we went in her closet. There were piles of clothes and shoes. They were all organized.

"Hey, maybe you should wear the dress I got you for Christmas."

"I doubt it. It's going to be thirty degrees on New Year's Eve, and it is a sleeveless dress."

Nelly picked out a white sweater for herself. She said she was also going to wear black leggings and a pink skirt with her boots. For me, she picked out a pink sweater and white leggings with glittery brown boots. Then she gave me a pair of big silvery owl earrings and a sparkly blue necklace. She picked out a heart-shaped pink necklace and heart-shaped pink earrings. She gave me the ones with the smaller size.

"Um, Nelly?"

"Yes, Leah?"

"I don't really want to wear this. I'm sorry."

Nelly looked offended. "Please!"

I heaved a sigh. "All right, I will, I will."

"Thanks, Leah!" She hugged me.

Aw, great.

Chapter 23: The Ball Drop

Uncle Ray was in a hurry the day before New Year's. That day, we were supposed to stay in a hotel near where the ball drop was going to take place. We thought that we could walk there very quickly from our hotel and beat the crowd before it became huge or left us with little room to watch that amazing ball drop site. Plus, we could explore that area of New York during the day and watch the memorable ball drop at night.

We drove to an awesome hotel. That day, we played Monopoly, walked around New York, and ordered room service while watching movies. Jelly didn't come. He was with a dog sitter.

The next day, on New Year's Eve, I woke up early. I realized I would have to go back home in two days. Well, I did stay in New York for almost three weeks. So that's good.

Aunt Denise was also the only one up, sipping tea. She told me she absolutely hated coffee.

"Good morning, Leah. Anything bothering you?" Aunt Denise looked up from her book titled *The Book Crook*. Interesting title for a book, I thought. She seemed to be a voracious reader, like me, probably another thing in common between her and me.

"No, well, yes. I don't really feel like going home, as I told you earlier."

"Don't you want to put your family back together? Make the FYF?" I felt like Aunt Denise was trying to say something else, but she wanted me to find out on my own.

"It feels like a whole lot of pressure on me. I mean, it's like it's *my* responsibility to make everything right." I slumped down on the chair on the mini dining table. My hair was sticking up, and I wasn't wearing glasses, so I couldn't see my aunt's beautiful face clearly.

Aunt Denise said in a candid pitch, "Maybe it is your responsibility to make things right. But I know you won't give up." That doesn't sound like Aunt Denise.

I stared at my aunt. "Great. Do I really have to—"

"What's great?" Nelly was up, rubbing her eyes. Eric was now up. The only one who was sleeping was Uncle Ray, still snoring like a pig.

When Uncle Ray finally woke up, we went to the lobby for breakfast. I had to wear what Nelly told me to wear. She made me brush my short hair. I had to do eighty-three strokes! Then she told me to apply a small amount of her perfumed lip balm to make my dried lips look shiny and smooth. I also applied some face lotion to give a nice glow to my face. My hair was silky and knot-free for the first time. They smelled like fresh strawberries because I used Nelly's special hair shampoo.

I looked like a different person. Nelly probably gave me a mini makeover.

At five o' clock, we headed from our hotel and walked to Times Square. Some people were there. We stood on the first row for a *long* time until the show started! And guess who performed, the one and only Emma Donatello! Also lots of other singers.

"Emma! I love you!" Nelly yelled. I did too. The camera swiveled toward *us*! Nelly and me! We made this funny face. Then the news crew faced the other way. We giggled. But I will never giggle like a girly girl again. It's not meant for me.

I had a blast. I didn't even notice my legs ached like crazy until after the ball drop.

"It's eleven forty-five!" Uncle Ray and Eric said at the same time.

"I hope this year turns out good," I muttered.

I asked everyone what their New Year's resolution was. Aunt Denise said it was to have more free time, Eric said it was to get accepted for an internship, Uncle Ray said it was to lose weight and be fit, and Nelly said she wanted to go on a national cooking competition. Then Nelly asked what *my* New Year's resolution was. I knew what it was. So did Aunt Denise. It was to make my family closer.

But to Nelly I said, "Start a, um, toenail collection?"

"Wha—" But Nelly was interrupted by

TEN!

NINE!

EIGHT!

SEVEN!

SIX!

FIVE!

FOUR!

THREE!

TWO!

Nelly covered her ears.

ONE!

HAPPY NEW

YEAR!

The ball dropped, and the confetti started.

I'm pretty sure after that I became 50 percent deaf.

"My ears!" I screeched.

Eric said, "Leah, they're not going to hear you."

Nelly nodded. "Unfortunately. They're going to make your throat sore."

Uncle Ray added, "And try to crush you."

After fifteen minutes, people started to move.

"Oh goodness, it's like a zombie apocalypse out here," Aunt Denise said.

We waited for about an hour so we could squeeze through the crowd. When we reached the hotel, my whole *body* ached.

"I'm never standing so long like this again," Nelly said, drinking a big mug of hot cocoa.

"Never *ever* standing like this again," I said.

"Hey, Leah, I think three days from now there is this convention called FanGirls Unite. You can make your own booth of the thing you're a fan about. Ours can be Emma Donatello," Nelly said eagerly.

"That sounds great—wait, oh, I'm going back home in two days."

Nelly frowned. "Really? Honestly, Leah, I forgot you didn't live here."

"Me too," I stated in agreement.

Chapter 24: Good-bye, New York City

As I repacked my bags the day I was going back to Cherry City, I couldn't help but think about what I had to do back home.

These were the steps I wrote.

Plan A.

Step 1: Make FYF

Step 2: Tell my family how much they yell

Step 3: They realize themselves and stop

Plan B.

Step 1: Compliment my siblings

Step 2: Try to spend more time with them

Step 3: My siblings become my friends and I tell them to behave well and they listen

If this works, I'll have peace at last!

You may not think that's a lot of work. But not if you have Allison and Fred to deal with, especially Allison.

I went to the main hall. Uncle Ray and Nelly would drop me to the airport. Meanwhile, I hugged Eric and Aunt Denise.

"Bye, Leah," Eric said.

"Bye, dear," Aunt Denise said, giving me a big hug. Then she whispered something, *"Don't give up."*

I tried to say something, but there was a lump in my throat. Nelly, Uncle Ray, and I headed out the door. I looked back at Aunt Denise, who stood there at the doorway, those beautiful sparkly raven-black eyes squinting at me as if it were trying to say good-bye and "I love you, I'm so glad you came. Come back soon." I looked at her with my ugly brown eyes, looking at her the same way except I was saying, "I love you, I'm glad I came. Please make me come back soon."

The weather was pleasant the day I left, total opposite of the day I came. I thought of all the fun and good times. I sighed.

We drove to the airport in total silence. When we arrived, Uncle Ray and Nelly stayed with me until we met the flight attendant at the security checkup.

As a good-bye, I hugged Uncle Ray, and then I turned to Nelly. Her hair was uncombed and loosely open, and she was just wearing jeans, shirt, and boots. I smiled at that change. I hugged her, and she hugged me.

Nelly said, "Thanks for making me realize that wearing simple clothes is okay. And insulting others is not the way to have fun but that's called bullying. I now know what a true friend means, and Hannah is definitely not one of them."

I nodded. "No problem."

"Bye," I said. An empty feeling was in my stomach. Maybe that's because I didn't eat much at all that day. But I'm pretty sure it was because I was sad.

"Bye, maybe next time we can see you in Cherry City," Nelly said.

"See you, my wonderful niece," Uncle Ray said.

I turned away. The flight attendant hoisted my luggage, and I walked, not daring to look back because I'd cry. And I hated it when I cried.

Chapter 25: Back to My Family

The airplane ride was worse than when I came to New York. When I was coming to New York, I knew I would just have fun. But when I was going back, I knew I'd have stupid stuff to deal with.

I read a bit of *Family Forever: Not in My World*.

> October 1, 1985
>
> Dear Diary,
>
> Today I'm still thinking of how to get my family to notice me and be perfect.
>
> I was eating chocolate, and a perfect idea hit me. What if I do something bad?
>
> So the next day at school, I—

I stopped reading.

The flight was delayed two hours. It was so sickening. Finally, I arrived in the evening. And guess who came to pick me up? *Nobody!*

My parents probably forgot I was coming home. Really? Were they already used to life without me? The flight attendant had to call my parents, and then forty-five minutes later, my mother came and picked me up.

"Hello, Leah," Mom said. She looked even more tired than usual.

The attendant made Mom sign some forms, and we left to go home.

When we finally arrived, Mom said sorry about picking me up late. I replied that it was okay, even though it wasn't to me. She hugged me.

When I opened the door, guess who came to me? Daisy.

Stupid Allison! She didn't even care to stay in Daisy's room, and she was supposed to babysit while Mom had to pick me up. Daisy cried a lot first but started smiling as soon as she saw me. Mom asked, "So how was your trip?"

I told her the summary of my trip. Of course I didn't tell her about the FYF or Plan B.

I went to my room. Same old, same old. Allison opened her bedroom door for a second and then slammed it.

"What's up with her?" I asked Mom.

"Her trip to Mexico didn't turn out so well. Sondra's mother called me and said that she ran away from the hotel and started driving with another eighteen-year-old girl, Brianna Baxter. Then, Brianna ditched her in the middle of the road. Allison called me, and Sondra's mother found her and yelled at her. Sondra's family didn't want her to stay with them anymore, so the next day, Allison came back."

Fred came out of the door. "Mom, where's my cologne—oh, hi, Leah. Did you meet Eric?"

Eric and Fred were good friends when they were little. That was all he cared about. I was not offended.

Kind of.

"Yeah, I met him," I replied.

"Cool." Then he went to the bathroom to get ready for a sixteenth birthday party. *Again.*

Teenagers. Probably aliens from another planet.

"Okay, your father is coming home from work in an hour. I've got to run some errands at the grocery store. So can you watch Daisy?"

"Sure. I guess."

"If you're hungry, I got some chicken nuggets for you. It's on the counter. Warm it on the microwave if it is cold, sweetie. Oh, and how's everyone in New York?" Mom was showing a little interest.

"They're good."

"Okay, bye." She left.

I was not hungry. I wanted to start Plan B. I would do both plans. I thought this one would work out better. I knocked on Allison's door.

"What?" she asked, opening the door. She didn't even ask how my trip was.

"Nothing, just wanted to talk. I came back from New York today, you know."

"One, I'm not a psychologist that you can talk to. And two, I really don't care if you came back from *Mars!*" My sister closed the door.

"I got you a top from New York!" Those words came out of my mouth quickly.

She opened the door a little and eyed me. Then Allison eagerly said, "For real?"

"Um, yeah. I'll only give you the top if we can do something together or at least talk."

"Okay, okay, just get me the top!" Allison replied.

I hurried to my room. What would I do? I had no top! My suitcase wasn't zipped very well, so when I actually knocked it over, some of my clothes fell over. Then I spotted something. Nelly's silver dress! It was long enough to be Allison's shirt. So I grabbed the dress and gave it to her.

"*Wow!*" Allison exclaimed when I gave her the dress—um—shirt.

"Can I come in?" I batted my eyelashes.

Allison raised her eyebrows. "Why do you want to come in? You never wanted to before."

"Well . . . I have a project at school due in March called, My Role Model. I picked you. So until March, I've got to write a seven-page report on my role model."

Allison blinked. Her silvery eye shadow shone bright. "You picked me?"

"Yes."

"Come in then!"

I went into Allison's room. It was painted red, and there was a bed, a vanity, and a big closet.

"Anyways, what do you have to write about—" Allison was cut short by a phone call. "Leah, I'm going to Stella's house. Fred's gone now, I think, so take care of Daisy."

"All right," I said. She left, and my plans were foiled.

Daisy was on the couch. "Hewwo bah, Lee!" she squealed when she saw me.

"Hi, Daisy." My stomach growled. I went to the kitchen. I didn't really like chicken nuggets, so I decided to go to Pete's. I guess I had to take Daisy with me, so I got her stroller, and we left.

When I went inside the room, Maria was scrubbing the counter, and Mr. Cortez was mopping the floor.

"Hello, Leah, I haven't seen you in a while!" Maria said gleefully.

"Hello, Ms. Karris," said Mr. Cortez. "Maria's told me a lot about you."

"Hi!" I said.

Maria spotted Daisy. "Aw! *She's so cute!* That must be Daisy. How old is she?"

"Thanks, she's two and a half. She's going to turn three in six months."

"Can I get you anything?" Maria asked.

"Sure. One medium pepperoni and sausage pizza, please. And for Daisy, just a small plain cheese pizza. And one medium rice and beans with salsa and guacamole." I was hungry.

"Okay. Eight forty-two, please."

"Oh dang, I left my purse at home! Wait, let me get it." I got Daisy's stroller and started to leave.

"Nah, Leah, it's okay," said Mr. Cortez. "You can give it to us later."

"Really? Thank you so much." Mr. Cortez went to the kitchen.

As I sat down with Daisy, Maria came and sat next to me. "So where have you been, Leah? I heard Allison saying that she was going to Mexico."

"I was in New York, visiting my cousins and aunt and uncle. I went by myself. It was *awesome!*"

Maria smiled. "Lucky. I had to stay here in the restaurant and clean."

I suddenly felt very bad.

"So where'd Allison go?" she asked curiously.

"Mexico."

"How was it? Did she have fun? Who'd she go with?"

"She went with Sondra Andreas and her family. She came back early because she left them and started driving with this other girl. Then Sondra's mother was angry and made her leave."

"Wow . . . that's bad."

"Yeah. Hey, Maria, is your father's real name Pete?"

"No, it's Miguel. We just said Pete because we liked Pete's Pizzeria."

"Why don't you name it Mexican Pizza Bistro?"

"Hey, I like that. But it costs a lot of money to do the paint on the building. We already put Pete's Pizzeria on it."

Mr. Cortez put the food on the table. Once again, I enjoyed it a lot. So did Daisy.

"Wow, thank you so much, Mr. Cortez. I'll come back soon to pay you back. Bye."

I left with Daisy back home. Mom's car was there. *Oh no!*

"Leah Karris!" Mom yelled when I entered. "Where in the world have you been? And where is Allison?"

"Allison is at her friend's house. I was just, um, taking a walk with Daisy."

Mom looked at me. "*Unbelievable!* Allison's going to be in big trouble. Why did you go out?"

"I was bored. And Daisy was getting fussy."

Mom sighed. "Inform me next time by calling me from the home phone." Then Mom got a call. "Dang. Allison's near Serene Lake! Can you believe it? I've got to pick her up from there! It's at least an hour drive from here to Serene Lake because of the traffic! Oh, and I have to go to work. Listen, Leah, I have to go. By the time I come back, your father and Fred might be home. Take care of Daisy."

She left *again*.

Hard to believe that this was the day I came back from a two-week trip.

I mean, I get the whole Allison thing, but Mom could've canceled work.

I put Daisy in her crib. Then I sat on the couch. The home phone rang. I answered it.

"Hello? Is this Steve Karris?" a voice said. The voice sounded serious and stern.

"Um, no. This is *Leah* Karris, Steve Karris's daughter. Who is this?"

"I'm Robert Jenkins, owner of Genetic Technology. I am the boss of Steve Karris. Also, Mr. Karris has not been picking up his phone. What is he dang doing? Is he here?"

"No. But if you have a message, I can tell—"

"Tell Karris that he is *demoted again*! He is lazy and—"

"Excuse me? What do you mean, Mr. Jenkins? Are you sure you know your facts?" I said, trying to keep my voice calm, but I was shaking with anger.

"Listen, young lady, you better keep quiet and be docile and act like a kid because you know nothing—"

"Listen, my father is hardworking and a good person! You, on the other hand, do no work at all and blame it on other people just because they don't pick up the phone. You—"

"Leah!" I heard my father's voice. "What are you doing? Is that Mr. Jenkins?" He grabbed the phone from me. "Mr. Jenkins?" Dad asked. "I am so sorry—"

"Shut up, Karris!" Jenkins barked. "You are suspended with *no* salary from this company until further notice!"

And the phone hung up. I was dead meat.

Chapter 26: The Patient, Calm, and Intelligent One

Dad gawked at me. "I am speechless, Leah. I'm just so disappointed." Then he left to his room, leaving me to feel guilty, mad, and sad all at the same time. First of all, I was trying to defend him, and he was disappointed? How rude! And second of all, I just came back from a two-week trip and no hello or hi? Even more rude!

Fred came home twenty minutes later. "Dad," he said. "I need to buy some supplies for a project for school."

Dad replied, "Oh, okay—actually I can't! I've been suspended from my company because some people have offended my boss with their rude talk!"

"*Stop!*" I shrieked. "I tried to defend you! And you're saying I'm being rude? Talk about hypocritical behavior!"

My father looked at me. "Young lady, go to your room. Don't dare talk to me like that."

Okay, so maybe I was a bit rude.

Okay, just medium-ish rude.

Okay, fine, maybe a lot rude.

But Dad was rude to me. Still, I shouldn't have said that.

Mom came home. Dad and Mom whispered to each other, and I could only make out a few words like "Leah" "Money" "What should we do?"

At dinner, which was cold leftovers of tuna salad, nobody talked. Nobody cared that I came back from New York today.

"Leah, come here," Dad said. "I want you to talk to Mr. Jenkins and say sorry. I don't know if that will make any difference to my job situation, but I just want him to know that we are all sorry."

"'Kay, Dad, sorry," I said. "I'll talk to him."

The reason I had to be so composed was because my family was in chaos. I was trying hard to be the patient, calm, and intelligent one.

Chapter 27: Report Card Day

Before I knew it, I was in school again, listening to Mrs. Albright's lectures. I was a bit at peace since I called Mr. Jenkins, who said my father was at least back in the company but in the original spot he was before since I apologized.

"Anyway, class, today we will be learning about manners. Your report cards will be going home today. I mentioned some behavior issues that a few of you have," Mrs. Albright said, eyeing me. "We will be listening to a presentation by William Hartman, Angela's father."

Angela spoke, "My father is a very sophisticated man. Just like his name. William Jacob Spacing Hartman II is my father's fancy name! So is my name, Angela Condell Hartman, and so is my mother's, Susanne Stephanie Dawson Hartman!" She was acting as if they were a royal family.

At lunch break, Dustin Ortega said to Angela, because she kept on talking about her family's fanciness, "Names do not make a person good, it's their actions and personality." Dustin had super curly blond hair and very dense blue eyes. He was always wise. I figured I needed to learn from him. I couldn't catch everything he said, though.

"How dare you? My family happens to own a lot of money. We have a pizza place in Cherry City, San Francisco, and San Jose!" I heard Angela snap.

"You're going a little off topic," I jeered. "He never said anything about your family's money—"

"*I'm telling on both of you!*" Angela said before she burst into tears. Fake tears, I believe.

A yard duty standing a little behind saw Angela "crying."

"What's the matter?" she asked.

"They are saying my family is not good and do not have a good personality and behavior! They also say I am poor!"

"Who's they?" the yard duty asked.

Angela pointed to Dustin and me.

"What is the meaning of this?" the yard duty said.

"Angela's lying! We didn't even say anything about—" I started.

"We were explaining about life," Dustin replied calmly.

"Is that so?" the yard duty remarked.

"Yes, miss, we were. People in the world need to learn about the other side of the world. Millions of people are starving and have illnesses every day, and if you have decent money, then donate to the needy instead of boasting about it. Names and money do not show a person's character. Behaviors and actions do—"

"All right, Mr. Wise Guy. Listen to me, I don't want anyone saying anything to anyone else or if they make people cry. Understood?"

"Mrs. Person-Who-Doesn't-Want-to-Listen-to-Good-Morals, can you please listen to him? It seems you need to learn something." I couldn't resist opening my big mouth.

"*Excuse me?* How dare you!" she said, shocked. "What disturbing children!" Then she stormed away.

Angela gave me a very dirty look and left.

Dustin still had a calm face. "Well, I'll be going," he said. "Bye, Leah."

I smiled as a good-bye. I went to the recess area. I saw Zoe Hawk with her big group of friends, the boys who played sports and girls on the monkey bars. I sighed. I decided to read some of Family Forever: Not in My World.

> I went to my classroom and put a bottle on the chair of my mean teacher, Madam Pin. "All right, worms! Turn to page hundred and ninety in your arithmetic workbooks!" And she sat down on the chair, and it made a

farting noise. Everyone laughed like lunatics.

"*Who did this?*" roared Madam Pin.

"*Me, madam*," I said, still smirking.

"*You! You little worm! To Headmistress Helena's office now!*"

And, boy, was I in trouble. I kept on laughing. Father and Mother were not pleased, and I had to do extra chores at home, and I had to help clean and do detention at school for a month.

After that, Mother and Father didn't give me much attention.

~SP

The bell rang. I quickly went to line up. Zoe Hawk was wearing a dress, and everyone was gathering around to see it. Zoe's hawk like eyes stared at me. "Hello, Leah. Nice look!" Everyone laughed since I was wearing a torn red sweatshirt and my hair was sprouting up like Frankenstein's bride.

"At least I don't have to put on lots of makeup to look decent," I snapped. Zoe did a death glare at me.

A girl asked, "Zoe, where'd you go for winter break?"

"Oh, I went to Los Angeles. But no biggie," Zoe said, with a hint of modest bragging. "Where did *you* go, Leah?"

"New York City. Flew by myself as an unaccompanied minor," I answered.

"Sure you did. Prove it on Monday, since it's the weekend," Zoe replied. "And if you want proof I went to Los Angeles, here's a picture." She showed me a picture of her near the Hollywood sign.

"Deal," I said confidently.

"Come on!" a voice said. I recognized it to be Dustin Ortega's. "Leah, are you actually going to do what they say?"

Zoe snapped, "None of your business, Justin Ortooga!"

"Zoe, for once, you're saying something true and sensible," I snapped too. I was annoyed.

Dustin shrugged. "Okay, Leah, if you want to do it that way."

I thought about it for a moment. Who cares about what Dustin says? I need to prove that I went to New York.

Mr. Hartman's presentation was horrible and boring. A slug could've given a better presentation -or lecture. He talked about "manners" and "respecting others"! It drove me "crazy"! And he kept looking at me when he did! Does he not know about social politeness?

I just couldn't shut my big mouth again. I burst out, raging."Excuse me, Mr. Hartman!" He raised his eyebrows. "I respect people by their behavior, not age. Also, you shouldn't look at people too much. It's not good *manners*."

Mrs. Albright was fuming after hearing my unexpected comments about Mr. Hart-mean – oh ! Hartman.

I think I speak my mind too often and that's getting me into trouble many times. Maybe I should start biting my tongue to zip my unstoppable mouth.

Mrs. Albright gave me a detention slip, and I had to go sit outside until the next period. So after school, I went to Mrs. Lean, who was talking on the phone. I waited. She noticed me but kept on blabbering. After fifteen minutes, I said, "Excuse me?"

Mrs. Lean shouted, *"Can't you see I'm on the dang phone?"*

I kept quiet for about ten more minutes. "I have detention—"

"Shut your mouth, kid!" she yelled. Then she hung up eleven minutes later. "Yeah, what do you want, eh?"

"I have detention."

Mrs. Lean laughed. "Can't stand a day without detention? Get in the detention room. I'm not going to go in there. And if I hear a peep, I'll give you an invitation for three weeks of detention."

I rolled my eyes. Thirty minutes later, I ran out of the detention room to go to my house.

When I arrived at my isolated block, I trudged to my front door and opened it wide. Nobody was there but Allison. "Great. Plan B, here I come!"

Allison was on her phone. "Yeah, so Sondra Andreas is such a wimp, right?"

I decided not to disturb her for the meanwhile. I went to get the mail, and I found my report card. I opened it right away.

Name: Karris, Leah

Class: Fifth Grade, Albright, Louise

Math: B+

English: A-

History: B+

Science: B

Writing: A

Comments: Leah is a good writer, but she needs to learn how to behave in the classroom and stay calm instead of being a little "misbehaving" with other students and teachers. She will get Academic Honor Roll but not Role Model Citizen Award.

"She could've been more direct that I'm the rudest in her class." I also saw Fred and Allison's report cards. Fred got all As, but Allison got three Cs, one F, and one D.

Allison came outside. When she saw her report card, she was fuming. "You twerp! You completely invaded my privacy!"

I said, "I'm sorry—"

"Shut up! Get inside now!"

There goes Plan B, I thought.

Allison slammed her door shut. I knew I was in hot water.

Fred came home ten minutes later. I decided to bond with him. "Hello, Fred!" I said excitedly.

"Um, hi, Leah," he said, putting his bag down.

"I checked your report card. I know I shouldn't have. Sorry about that, but you got all As!"

"I know."

"So, um, do you want to do something, since its Friday?"

"I don't know, I'm busy." He seemed surprised, like he forgot he was my brother. My eyes swelled with tears, and I didn't know why. I cried a bit. I remembered the days when Fred, Allison, and I used to play and laugh. I absolutely hated it, and when I tried to stop, I kept hiccupping.

"Leah," Fred said. "What's wrong?" He looked at me like I was stupid.

"I-I don't know." I was angry at myself for being so emotional.

"Do you really want to spend time with me?" he asked.

"I do. Even with Allison."

"With Allison?"

"Yeah, with Allison."

"Okay, I'm going to ask her. Wish me luck to see the Wizard of Oz—I mean Allison."

I laughed. "But she's mad at me. I looked at her report card."

"I'll talk to her." Fred knocked on Allison's door, and I went to my room and basically collapsed on my bed. I guess Fred wasn't that bad. Not bad, just an idiot.

Daisy was sleeping in her crib, and there was a note on my desk.

Leah, I'll be back by five, and your father will be back six, and Allison and Fred should be home. Love you.

—Mom

Fred came in my room about twenty minutes later. Allison came along.

"Hello, Allison. I'm sorry for looking at your report card. I won't do it next time," I apologized. "Can we just be like we were before, the three of us?"

Daisy woke up and whimpered. Before we come back from school, Mrs. Franklyn watches her for ten dollars an hour.

"Don't forget Daisy," Allison said, smiling.

Chapter 28: It Worked!

On Monday, I showed Zoe a picture of me, Nelly, Aunt Denise, Eric, and Uncle Ray at the Statue of Liberty.

Zoe replied, "Big whoop. Don't have to be such a bragger, Leah." Then all the group murmured "Yeah."

I was so shocked that some people could be that stupid. "Um, you told me to bring the picture to show you so I can prove that I went to New York."

Zoe and her group were walking away. "Were you saying something, Leah?" Zoe sneered.

Oh my gosh! That girl was just nuts.

Dustin Ortega stood facing me. "I'm not going to say 'I told you so' because it's ignorant and it has no point—"

"Enough, Wise Guy, stop being nosy," I snapped and walked away. Then I felt guilty. Was I too harsh? No, no way. It's none of his business.

When I came home, Allison and Fred were both there with popcorn. "Hey, Leah, we're just watching a movie, come join," Fred said. I readily agreed. Ever since the previous weekend, the three of us had been bonding. Kind of.

Allison was still arguing with Mom and Dad and still wore excessive makeup. Fred skipped dinner with Mom and Dad and still went out a lot. But when they were with me, they were great. The next part of my plan was to tell Allison and Fred to behave better with Mom and Dad. I had to do it in a way that they wouldn't be offended.

Fred went to go to the bathroom. Allison saw me thinking densely. "Anything bothering you, Leah?" Allison asked as she put popcorn in her mouth.

I told her about Dustin Ortega and Zoe Hawk.

"Zoe Hawk?" Allison said. "I know her brother! Jared Hawk! He's in my history class! I hate that dude! As for Justin—"

"Dustin," I corrected.

"As for *Dustin* Ortega, tell him to back off. It's your business. Are you friends with him?"

"No, not really," I said.

"Who are your friends?"

"Well, I don't have many," I admitted. "But there's a girl named Sally Lee who was my friend, kind of. She moved six months ago."

"You have no friends?" Allison questioned, shocked.

"Well, yeah, if you put it that way," I said, annoyed.

"Well, I knew you were dumb, but not that dumb that you have no friends!" Allison joked.

"Shut up, Allison!"

"Don't be mad, twerp. I have to be blunt with you. Stop being shy."

"Whatever." I looked back at the TV screen and plopped buttery popcorn into my mouth.

Allison shrugged. I decided to say a little something.

"Allison, why do you get so angry at Mom and Dad sometimes?" When I saw an angry look on her face, I quickly said, "I mean, I know you wouldn't get mad for no reason. There must be a valid reason." Her face did soften.

"Well, sometimes they don't let me go to the most awesome *parties* of the year! Like Jenny Berry's party. And Stella Fire's. And Charlie Puck's—"

"Any other reason?" I interrupted.

"I don't know. Sometimes, I just can't control myself, I just get mad for petty little reasons. I'm not like that."

"That's hard to believe, Allison, if you keep behaving like that. You're a nice, sweet girl. And why do you use so much makeup?"

"I feel insecure. I feel *ugly*."

"You're not. Just put a little bit of makeup and let your natural beauty shine more."

Allison beamed. "I guess so, Leah, thanks."

It worked, it worked, it worked!

Chapter 29: The FYF

And the results did come. When Mom accidentally burnt Allison's toast the next day at breakfast, Allison didn't get super mad like she usually would. She was about to yell, but then she saw me looking at her. "I'll just have yogurt," she said.

But they did fight sometimes. Sometimes more, sometimes less.

FYF time!

I observed and wrote whenever I had time:

FAMILY YELLING FLIP CHART

February 16th

Who fought: Mom and Allison fought with each other; Fred and Dad.

Why they fought: Mom and Allison fought because Allison was upset about her bedding;

Fred and Dad fought because Dad was sick of Fred eating so much sugar. Then the topic of the fight led to Fred wanting a new computer!

How much time they fought: Mom and Allison fought thirty-five minutes; Fred and Dad fought thirty minutes!

February 22nd

Who fought: Fred and Allison.

Why they fought: Who wanted the TV remote, then the topic of the fight led to Allison's grades and Fred's socks.

How long they fought: One hour and five minutes.

March 3rd

Who fought: Mom and Fred.

Why they fought: Fred came back an hour late.

How long they fought: Thirty minutes.

March 9th

Who fought: Mom and Dad.

Why they fought: Dad didn't talk at all since he came back from his business trip.

How long they fought: One hour and twenty-three minutes.

March 18th

Who fought: Dad and Allison.

Why they fought: Allison wore too much makeup for Dad's liking.

How long they fought: Thirty minutes.

I stopped after that. I figured that was enough. And yes, I was a bit of a hypocrite for not recording my own fights. But I barely fought those times. I had to do one more thing before presenting this to the family.

Fred was on his computer. "Leah, I'm busy right now." He didn't look up when he said that. I didn't ask why he knew it was me coming in his room.

"I know. But, Fred, I really, really need to talk to you."

Fred looked up. "Okay, but make it quick. What's up?"

"Why don't you like going out with us anymore? Why do you skip dinner and stuff with us?"

Fred didn't have any expression on his face. He said firmly, "I'm sixteen, almost seventeen in two months. I want to have fun with my *friends*."

"I know. But you are going to college soon, and you can have all the fun with your friends then. But you can't with your family."

Fred stared at the wall. "I never thought of that."

"You should." Then, sounding like Dustin Ortega, "Your family will not last forever. I, Allison, Mom, and Dad are not going to be around for a long time. You aren't either. You are blessed with a family, and you keep wasting all the time you could be with your family." I didn't say it as good as Dustin would, though.

"Leah, you are right. But Mom and Dad are busy. That's not my fault."

"You are extremely correct. Can't we convince them? I'm sure they understand. They may not spend time with us as much anymore, but they still love us."

Fred actually smiled. "You are totally right." He might be saying that to get me out of his room, but I thought it was quite genuine.

I walked to the hall and saw Mom cooking, and then Daisy spilled milk, so she was running to get a mop.

"Mom, you need to relax," I noticed.

"Oh, well if you can find someone who can do all the chores, I will! And maybe if you can do the laundry!" Mom snapped.

"We can help you, and I'll try doing the laundry. Life doesn't last forever, you know, so you have to enjoy it, not stress."

"I don't know."

I was not sure which one she didn't know: life not lasting forever or us helping her.

Chapter 30: Family Vacation!

The next evening at dinner, I was serving steamed potatoes. Fred, Mom, Dad, and Allison were smiling. "What's up with the happy faces?" I asked, taking a bite of meat loaf. And if Fred was there, something really big happened.

"*Family vacation!*" they all said at the same time.

I literally spit out my food. "What? Really?"

"Yes," Mom said. "Fred told us about it. He said you were his inspiration. Okay, Fred didn't say it like that . . . Okay, erm, where was I? Oh, yes, you are absolutely right, Leah, that we don't spend time much anymore."

"And fight a lot," I added and ran to get the FYF.

I showed them my flip chart. "Oh, we fight *this* much?" was Mom's comment. Dad's was "What?

How the heck did I not notice?" Fred's was "I was expecting this." Allison said, "Wow, great job! We made number 1 Fighting Family Award!"

"Leah, thank you for making us realize this," Mom said. Everyone else muttered "Thanks."

Dad got a second serving of potatoes when he said, "We're going to San Diego next weekend. We'll start on Friday at five a.m., and then we'll stay there for the weekend. The flight is at seven o' clock. Since it is a forty-five-minute drive to the airport and we have a lot of airport stuff to do, we have to wake up early. You guys have to skip school. I convinced Mr. Jenkins to give me a leave for a day."

Everything was literally great. My hard work paid off!

At least I thought so.

Chapter 31: A Fun Day at San Diego

That Friday, we started at 5:30 a.m. because we took a long time to get ready. We meaning Allison. Our flight was at 7:00 a.m, and we barely made it to the airport. The plane ride was short but turbulent. Allison kept groaning and whining until Mom told her to be quiet. I finished all of *Family Forever: Not in My World*. The last few pages in the book described how SP kept doing wacky stuff to get attention and finally gets it when SP breaks his or her arm. Then the arm gets healed, and SP's family is back to doing who knows what.

It just ended there. I didn't like the ending because it was kind of stupid.

We arrived at two thirty because of the traffic. We were staying at a hotel. We had a partial view of the ocean. It was so beautiful.

We rested and then went to the beach. I went a bit into the water. It was chilly, since it was winter, but was still pleasant. Soon I was doing a backstroke. Allison and Fred tried to bodysurf. I tried it too, and I had lots of fun even though I kept falling off.

We splashed water at one another. Mom, Dad, and Daisy were sitting on the sand. Then we had ice cream. We then went to Seaport Village to shop. I didn't get much except a shell necklace, but Allison got a ton of stuff.

At night, we went to the Big Bay and had dinner.

The day was perfect. Too bad it didn't last long.

Chapter 32: Going Downhill

I was reading a book when Allison asked me where the sunscreen was and I told her it was in my bag. A couple of minutes later, she said, shocked, "What is this?" and Mom, Dad, Fred, and I went to go check.

She was holding my Plan A and Plan B paper.

"Oh, that," I said, laughing. "That was just my plan to get this family back together."

"No," Fred snapped. "You lied."

"What?" I gasped. I was taken aback.

"You lied about wanting us to spend time. You just wanted 'peace,'" Allison barked. "I can't believe this." She probably read one of my lines from the plan: *If this works, I'll have peace at last!*

"Um, I didn't mean—"

"You toyed with our emotions!" Fred cried. "I actually believed you, Leah! But you don't even care about this family! Peace? It says right here, '*Become friends with my siblings and convince them to behave better*.'"

"I-I'm—" I was struggling for words.

"Oh, be quiet!" Allison scolded. "Don't even talk to us. All this was just a staged act. Oh yeah, that report thing on 'Who is your role model?' was probably baloney too. I thought we were actually friends!"

"We are, Allison," I said. "I actually did want to be friends with you. And the report . . ." I couldn't complete my sentence.

"That seems hard to believe," Fred snapped.

I got really angry. "*Excuse me? Do you know how hard I worked to make this family back together? I was so sad, I had so many difficulties, and now you're like, 'Oh, you played with our emotions.' That is so wrong! I did want to be your friend, I* wanted to make everything right, and now you're making it worse, Fred and Allison. You just are!"

"Kids—" Dad said.

Fred replied in the same tone, "*Oh, come on, Leah! Difficulties? You? Do you have seven tests on the same day then go home and do chores then keep doing the same thing over and over? The only reason I go out is to actually enjoy myself for once!*"

"*Stop—*" Mom said.

Allison yelled, "*Shut up, both of you! You both don't have any difficulties! Every day I get teased and taunted by Tess Ballinger, who says that I'm ugly and I have to keep buying makeup to fit in! I'm ridiculed all the time.*"

Dad was now fuming. "*Do you have to go to work eight hours a day, sometimes work overtime, pay the bills, and then make enough money to go on vacations such as this?*"

Mom looked even angrier than all of us. "*Do you have to wake up at five a.m., then make breakfast, then feed Daisy, then wash her, then go to work, then do the housework, then do errands, then make a big dinner?"*

Daisy woke up and was yelling, *"Stop! Stop! You guys stop!"*

We were all quiet. Allison and Fred left the hotel room without a word. Mom and Dad said they were going to the lobby.

I was alone and feeling guilty, especially for Mom. Mom did so much stuff. As for Dad, him too. And Fred. I felt Allison's problem wasn't a big deal. I was a gossip target for weeks, and they threw my *clothes* into the trash can, for Pete's sake!

Everything was getting horrible. Then I felt angry again. Why the heck were Fred and Allison getting so touchy and emotional on a stupid little thing? If they wanted to do so much drama, why didn't they join a soap opera or something?

Although I was kind of dramatic too, but I was telling the truth. All I attempted to do was to make everyone happier.

Things were going back to square one. But what could I do about it? I tried so hard, and this was where we ended up again. I was not trying again, I decided. *I give up.*

And I did give up.

Chapter 33: Realizing

"We're canceling the rest of our trip," Dad announced. "There isn't much more to see. Also, Mr. Jenkins said that there was an emergency at the office. I called an airline and booked tickets for an early flight So go pack."

Nobody said one word. We got a cab then drove to the airport. "Be careful when you cross these streets, near the airport" Mom said to me.

I was sulking while I walked out of the cab. How did things get so downhill so fast? I thought this was going to be a fun—

"*Leah!*" Allison cried, pushing me and herself out of the way of a truck that was going to run over me in seconds. "Are you okay? Are you hurt?"

"No, I'm fine," I replied, amazed. "Thanks, Allison, you saved my life."

"Did you expect me to let you die?" Allison asked but sounded angry. "Even Mom told you to be careful! *You could've gotten killed!*"

"I'm sorry, Allison, but thank you!" I said, giving her a hug.

Mom, Dad, and Fred came near me quickly. "Sweetie, are you all right?" Mom asked.

"I wasn't going to be, but Allison came and saved me!"

I was going to point to Allison, but she was already gone, walking toward the entrance. "Allison, wait!" I shouted, running after her.

We all finally caught up with Allison at the airport shop. "Hi, can I have a Band-Aid?" she asked the lady at the counter.

"Sure," the lady replied, giving her a pack of Band-Aids.

"How much—"

"You got . . . hurt?" I said shockingly.

Allison turned and raised her eyebrows. "Yeah, so?"

Then I noticed a big scrape on her left arm.

Mom seemed worried. "How did you get that, Allison?"

"It's not a big deal, Mom," Allison said, but she didn't sound all rude; she sounded quite soft. "I just tripped and cut myself on a rock when you guys were talking to Leah."

"Oh dear," Mom said.

"You got hurt for me?" I asked.

"Not really, I got hurt after I saved you," Allison snapped. "I'm not that bad that I'd let you get injured, twerp."

"I know," I lied.

Allison glared at me.

"Okay, maybe I didn't know that you care that much for me."

"Listen, twerp, anyone would've done that," Allison said.

I remembered a movie when the girl said to her friends, "We all have our difficulties." Then all the friends agreed, and then they did a group hug. One of them said, "We're all friends again! We need to respect one another since we understand difficulties in everyone's lives."

Maybe it would work in this scenario?

I did exactly what the girl did and looked down at the ground. "We all have our difficulties. We should respect one another since we all have some bad stuff in our life."

Allison got me on this one. "This isn't a Disney movie and we agree then we become all mushy-mushy and nice and we hug."

"I was kind of hoping it was," I snapped. "At least movies have happy endings and solutions to problems."

"We don't have any problems," Mom said.

"Yes, we do!" I replied. "We never spend time. We just fight. This trip made me realize we can never get better."

They all looked bewildered.

"Yes, we are a fighting family!" I said again.

"All families are like that," Fred said.

"Except *The Brady Bunch*," Dad pointed out.

I rolled my eyes.

"We can't show our love and affection all the time. Look at Allison, she showed her care for you when it mattered most," Mom stated earnestly.

"Plus, not all families have four members out of five eating breakfast and dinner," Dad said.

Fred did an awkward chuckle at that one.

Suddenly, I remembered Aunt Denise's eyes wanting to tell me something that day at the hotel. She wanted me to know that I didn't have to make things right. She gave me the *Family Forever* book for the message. After SP got her family's attention, it was no use! SP didn't like breaking his or her arm! And plus, when SP's arm got healed, her family was the same again! The last sentence in the book was "My family will remain my family. I hope you know that too." My family is just a family! Not a perfect one! Just a plain old family. Mom was right; you don't have to show your affection all the time. Allison loved me. And honestly, I felt like I had tried to fix my family for nothing. My family was already all right.

"I understand!" I shouted. Everyone was on their phones, waiting to board the flight, so they said nothing.

Suddenly, Allison said, "Mom, Dad, I'm sorry if I was ever rude to you. Leah did make me realize to stop that, and thanks for that. I'll try to stop wearing too much makeup. But I can't guarantee that I'll become all sweet and a perfect child."

"I never wanted you to be like that. I just don't want you to be upset all the time," Mom said.